BEYOND
HOME
A daughter's journey

ROBIN BOWER

Beyond Home
A daughter's journey

Copyright © Robin Bower 2014

ISBN: 978-0-9941913-0-4

www.robinbower.com.au

This novel is entirely a work of fiction. The names, characters and incidents portrayed in it are the work of the author's imagination. Any resemblance to actual persons, living or dead, events or localities is entirely coincidental.

Prologue

His breath came in short, sharp bursts, the rhythm of his heartbeat matching his footfall on the slippery path. The path was a track that had become overgrown with the plants of a jungle close to the city, far enough away to remain a secret, close enough to reach in less than a day. The canopy overhead teemed with birdlife, insects and familiar creatures he could hear but not see, but he could name them all. The chatter of birds and the clicking of insects kept the symphony of the forest alive. This canopy was home to an abundant living community, providing shade for growth yet, for him, as he pounded the path in wafer-thin sandals, this jungle was a curse. It shut him in, trapped him, blocked him.

The machete he had been given as a child had blunted against the thickness of the branches; he threw it to one side with a grunt remembering his father's words: 'Use only for defense, not in attack'. His father did not know the life he had led, was from another country, another world. This country with its tropical rainforests, mountains and beaches was both a treacherous and enchanting place, one which did not embrace difference. There was no need to turn his head to know they were close; he could feel them. Only two of them, but when he stopped running to listen, he could hear their feet catching up. He could hardly see the passage through the trailing vines; branches were constantly beating against his face. With bloody lips, and one eye closing from a quickly swelling cut, he could feel his tongue dehydrating. He could no longer moisten his lips with his own spit; the cracked edges were dried and red from a day without water. He coughed against the dryness to get some moisture back but it caused only pain.

Without water, he was dead. But if he could not outrun them, he was dead anyway. He knew there was a stream ahead — if he could find the monkey tree he would be safe, have refuge. It grew over a hollow cave nestled next to the creek providing water and shelter; he knew it was a good hiding place. How had they found him? No one knew about his secret place except her, but she would never tell.

The path took a sudden turn to the right — he missed his footing and plunged through the undergrowth, tumbling, falling, sand and mud in his mouth, his hair catching on jagged branches. His eyes shut against the pain — now he felt only the dark. He fought the pain — had to stay alert, to survive and warn the others.

His battered body tumbled down an embankment, gouging into every hole, hitting every tree stump and rock. He stopped rolling at the edge of the stream. He tried to move his arms and legs, to crawl into the shadows. The only movement he could manage was a twist of his head. The rest of him was spent. He lay there forcing his body to get up but it refused. They were at the top of the ridge now, shouting and looking down at his broken body. He lifted his head again, this time to free his face from the sludge, to breathe through his mouth. As he moved trying to raise himself, he saw the black boot at his right shoulder. It was a fine boot, military issue and polished to perfection under the adhering mud. The boot lifted and placed itself on his upper arm. The jolt of its force sent him further into the stream — he was floating on his back, incapable of movement. Pieces of blue sky appeared through the green of the canopy; its dappled light hurt his eyes. The pain was everywhere — not just his face with its bleeding cuts and monstrous swelling, but his legs, his arms, his heart. With one eye, he saw the raised rifle pointing directly at him.

He heard words addressed to someone else, and then came the words that were meant for him.

'You have done well, my friend. Now, do you wish to continue or get up and face us like a man? You know you can join us. There are always options.'

'You will never break me.' He turned his head then let it drop in the mud and reeds.

'Get up or I will shoot you in the head.'

The shot resounded in the river-formed valley. The echo was loud — the loudest sound he had ever heard. And would ever hear.

1

It was in need of rain, a flat landscape hit by the elements, unable to be destroyed. The struggling organisms that grew in the dirt had emerged to a life of hardship. Some were strong, hardy, thin to avoid the sun, and some were fleshy to hold water. Spinifex grass and low-lying scrub helped bind the sand and keep it in the ground. It was west of the verdant, cooler and more populated parts of Australia, less frequented by tourists, but home to more flies, sharks and jellyfish.

The white sun scorched the harsh, brown landscape and painted Eve's skin the color of the earth. She blended with her beloved dirt. Her hands were camouflaged while preparing the soil for the oncoming green. Although it would be slow this year, the Western Australian landscape had the capacity to come to life in her fingers. Her hands and face were mostly obscured by dust and sand as she cultivated, analysed and processed the organisms that defined her world. Her yellow hat hung down below her ears, all but obliterating her face — if anyone cared to look. No one seemed to notice her face. If someone did notice, they would have seen an olive complexion dirtied by the summer light. Her eyes were a deep blue, almost black, bordered above by a flash of sun-bleached strands covering her head in disarray. Smiling did not come easily to Eve. She struggled to recreate her muscles into the shape that other women found so useful in the years after turning 30. She had a slender straight body; her work on the land ensured its basic fitness, something she never thought about. She wore subdued colors and hadn't discovered that small ironing implement on the long board in her laundry, or the thin cylinder of pink resin for lip color. Her clothes looked tossed on, hair awry. Her nose had freckles, lines had formed on her forehead. She worked at blending into the background, cultivating anonymity the way she cultivated her gardens. She was in a garden now, not her own but one she loved. She did not yearn for her own, borrowed things did not come with a key she had to constantly keep watch over.

It was an Australian native garden, brimming with eucalyptus leaves and the white bark of tall gums. Her favorite grass tree stood resolutely, like a sentry guarding the entry to paradise. The tree was spiky and hard on the outside protecting the vulnerable softness beneath. Eve stroked the green length of the grass tree's sprout. She loved its slim, firm lines. Letting it go, she watched the rippling spikes connect and separate until they were calm again.

The garden belonged to an old woman who lived not far from Eve. Eve could not decline an offer to cultivate someone else's patch, even if it did distract her from her purpose. The purpose could wait but the growing creatures within the soil could not. The old woman's fingers were too gnarled to work on her natives and encourage them to grow. The bones in her back had crumbled so much she was now unable to move. Eve became her supple fingers and flexible body.

To others, Eve was a gardener. Gardening, as she had discovered, took a great deal of care, expertise and knowledge. Her own knowledge far exceeded that of most people who toiled the ground and helped nurture its beings. Her academic career had developed over many years, culminating in a doctorate in horticulture. This knowledge only helped her in the tending of the soil. Her studies were long term. Some called her a professional student, one who had excelled early in her career which had stalled to become a world of grass and roots.

A kookaburra hooted. She looked up to the gum tree's highest point, and saw the bird propped on a branch as if waiting its turn for the dentist. Its stare was constant. She noticed it didn't move the way other birds did. It was still as a pole — its eyes fixated on hers. She felt pressure in her neck, a sensation behind her eyes that grew to a throbbing. The color ebbed from her cheeks. The strange bird watched as her limbs gave way and she fell into the dirt.

*

Eve saw the once-tall man who had guided her through childhood. She called out to her father but he didn't seem to hear; he just looked ahead. He was a good man, worked hard, was solid and principled, never hit her, only yelled occasionally, always made up, knew he loved her, and she him. Was this what father/daughter relationships were supposed to be like? She'd seen fathers and daughters at the movies, Americans constantly saying 'I love you', words she could never say to her own father. Nor he to her.

Her childhood was not extraordinary. Australian beach and backyards, kittens in the wardrobe, large lawns and mulberry trees. Abalone shells on the river foreshore, big yellow hills, holidays on white sand, green water lapping at the shoreline. No one else.

She felt different from others her age. She was odd, didn't connect, didn't fit in. She amused herself by learning the botanical names of plants. She had an encyclopedic memory. She didn't read stories — and certainly not stories of adventure and horses. The adventures in her head were the adventures of the creatures that no longer walked the earth — the extinct creatures which now lived only in her memory. The best friends in Eve's childhood were *Tyrannosaurus rex* and *Hibiscus heterophyllus*. Loving the *T. rex* in those days was not one bit cool or clever. Just odd.

The man in her mind was looking at her. She remembered his routine — home at five, then his favorite chair. He was happy with simple things. He had been an athlete, had a flourishing career, so he'd said. What had he done in the first thirty years of his life before he had met her mother? The mother she had never met.

He used to like showing home movies taken at the back of the house. He would set up in the lounge room, organizing chairs to have a full view of the projector. Eve would scout for grey blankets to keep out the light fighting to get in through the stained glass window of the front door. He took so long setting up the film that she was past waiting. Finally, he would announce the start.

There was no drum roll but the lights went out and Eve's eyes were stuck to the screen. Inevitably, something went wrong and the screen burned and withered. What was that disappearing image? It was a rare one of her father smiling. He was walking down the grassy slope of the lawn outside the house. The frame stayed forever burnt but the image remained, surrounded by the raggedy black edge of its own destruction. There was the laughing girl with blonde curls, a young father smiling, delighting in the growth of his beloved child. Along with the pleasure, Eve felt a sadness that ebbed and flowed with the images. Sometimes her father looked at her in a strange way during these sessions, a look she didn't understand. She was in the frame on the screen, often, but always alone. At the zoo, on the lawn, up the mulberry tree dressed in bathers, and covered in mulberry juice, throwing the messy fruit at an unsuspecting dog. And, look there she is in nappies, crawling across the smoothness of the green expanse. There was more but her father began packing up the equipment, putting the leads back into boxes. He was serious at these showings. He was so intent on making it run smoothly that there was always a hitch.

'Don't touch that!' he bellowed to an inquisitive daughter.

Couldn't he play with her or act the fool at the beach? He never took her to the movies, the park or a school fête. Once they went to the coast but it rained, the car wouldn't start and they both got the flu. Sometimes he would go for Sunday drives. She remembered him getting so angry once that he picked up the birdbath from the side garden, and threw it at the fence. The fence smashed to fragments, but the birdbath was undamaged, but he had to go to bed for two hours. She couldn't remember what prompted his anger.

*

She felt supportive arms guiding her to a sitting position.

'You OK love?' said the voice. 'Here, drink this.'

She sat up, still dizzy, taking the glass and slowly sipping its cool freshness.

'Sorry — it must be the heat.'

'You should drink more water, my dear. You can finish the garden another time — you'd better get home.'

She sensed the old woman was right. She didn't know until later that the moment she fainted was the moment her father had died.

2

The day had begun as usual. The morning meeting at the office and interactions with colleagues Alex never saw in the real world. There was computer work and the inevitable paper jam of administration. His job was routine, predictable, constant. He knew the people he worked with, even liked them but he never invited them out or home for dinner or to see a movie. Nor did they invite him. He appeared not unfriendly but indifferent to them. He didn't come to morning teas, farewells, lectures, addresses by the general manager, divisional meetings, or lunches. He sat at his desk and ate tuna sandwiches every day in front of his computer. In the old days, he would do the same but in front of endless paperwork and tiers of files. With computers Alex could now attain the nirvana of the paperless office or at least attempt it. He never quite managed to get there as more paper evolved from printing every email, website link, and ministerial that came through every kind of technology. He couldn't see the logic to this, it was just protocol. Every piece of correspondence whether electronic or paper had to have an identification number and be filed according to subject. Not adhering to these protocols could certainly end in trouble and Alex, above all, wanted to avoid trouble. The realization that computers generated more paper than ever before made him smile. He remembered the simple life before computers but stopped himself in time as he normally did. He didn't have to pay for the paper or for the electricity bills so why should he worry? He engineered the process to become part of his job, added it to his list of tasks every day and accepted the fact that 80% of his job was recording what he did in his job. He thought of it more like a daily journal, one he was paid for. He recorded his times and tasks in a timesheet submitted every month to his supervisor, every file reference was recorded in another journal, every email into another which he filed in a suspension file on his desk. He didn't need to write his thoughts down or file them, they were the same every day – predictable, constant, routine. To himself anyway. He never tested them on anyone else.

Alex was always tired, especially by the end of the day when he looked forward to home. He hadn't built up a sweat by moving heavy logs or pieces of stonework or steel. He hadn't even expended much brain power in the work he did. All he knew was that he was tired in the morning and more tired in the afternoon when it was time to leave the office. But when he got home, he looked forward to going to work again the next day. He didn't cook, takeaway or pre-packaged dinners sufficed. He was not picky about food, never cared what he ate, it was merely to sustain him. He sometimes watched television programs that interested him — world wars, anything to do with history, European and Asian in particular. He loved the biographies of great war heroes. If television was bad, he read or did crosswords. He did not look forward to weekends, and found himself asleep for most of the 48 hours before Monday began again. With relief he would be at work, at his desk, looking at his files, and then he would want to be home.

He was unusually tired this day, making his way home in the normal way, driving the car that needed a service into the driveway of the house that was peeling and fragmented.

He had never thought his life would become this — the mundane, the routine. He'd had romantic visions of contentment and satisfaction, of a life well lived, and fatherhood fulfilled. He had wanted to guide the visions of the young through learning and development. His life had started so well. It was only the last thirty years that had passed quietly. He'd had a grand plan — once.

He had married. He knew she had loved him but had she loved their daughter? He was sorry in a way he had to take her from the country he had called home. She would never know how it felt to go to sleep under the stars, feel the tropical rain softening the skin on your face, the heat immerse your soul. He had loved every minute of his childhood in that tropical paradise. It was only as an adult that he realized paradise was flawed. It had not been easy for Eve in this new country, he could see that now. A father not willing to communicate, share his past, commit to emotional displays. He had tried but it seemed a lie, he couldn't even force it. He could only do what time had taught him. Quiet reflection on his past was all that he had. A past he thought he knew.

He had left her in the end. She had seemed all too willing to accept he had left with their child. She couldn't bring herself to leave her own country, even for her child. He realized he could not change the lives of a people, had given up. That was years ago. He was alone in his little house, without human stimulus and contact with the outside world. He had created an inner world for himself. But he still had Eve.

He edged his way around the car he'd parked too

close to the side of the garage. The door slammed hard hurting his ears. He walked towards the front door, crossing the straight red path that led there. His peripheral vision caught the overflowing post box. Unusual for a Tuesday, he thought. He didn't receive much mail. He could see the dark brown envelope peeking from the slot. The package was large with an unusual oriental stamp. A dizziness overcame him, he had to sit down.

Inside the house, sitting in his favorite chair and clasping the letter opener, he prized the package apart. He opened out the stiff wrapper, which held a small blue book in a hard cover. It looked like a child's diary — possibly a young girl's. He turned the first page, and his name jumped out. He knew immediately he was reading about his own life through someone else's eyes.

If his neighbor had heard the sounds emanating from the house, and if she had forged a friendship with Alex, she would have thought she heard someone crying, and have come in to offer sympathy. She would never have forgotten the sound of a man sobbing. But Alex's neighbor did not hear him weeping. No one heard his sounds of hurt, his outbursts of buried emotions that had risen to the surface.

The first page in the book contained a letter to Alex.

His heart was pounding, a tingling started in his fingers, his chest grew tight with pain. He wanted to scream but he found no voice to deafen the silence. He wanted to stop reading but his eyes kept on. They continued to absorb a world he had never contemplated, never knew existed, a treacherous world in which he had played an innocent part.

This life he had made for himself was a sham. As he released his grip on the small blue book, a stabbing pain hit him. Both hands gripped his chest, trying to stop the pounding pain surging down through his arms and neck.

In the diary he saw photos of himself as a baby he'd never seen before. Photos of a woman, Alexandra. She was saying she loved him, needed him but admitted to betraying him. And now she was saying come back to learn more of the truth? Come back to see a woman he had never known or loved, a place he now loathed and which had long terrified him. His father had lied. Love doesn't last forever.

His life had meant something in his early years, he'd made a difference, had a child, started a revolution. He had helped forge new lives for so many. But so many had died. Why had he kept everything a secret? He should have passed it on so it could never happen again. It was too late — he would pass away like the memories, like the children, like the fighting.

He tried to remember the face, it was a swirling pool of light with no definition. That face had made him stop. He wanted to remember. He wanted to tell Eve. Where would he start? It was time to end — not begin. There was no pain now. The book fell at his feet and opened.

'To my Alex, finally I have found you to tell you the truth that you so deserve to know ...'

3

As she closed the front door behind her and put her keys in the tray by the door, Eve heard a clattering in the kitchen and realized Roger was home. Early. Most days he would be home by eight. Two days a week he did extra shifts at the hospital — home at six for dinner and then out again at seven finishing at eleven, in bed by twelve. She didn't think of herself as a cook but managed the staple Australian favorites of spaghetti bolognese, Thai curry and Indian butter chicken. She loved cooking with the mixed spices of oriental flavors much to Roger's annoyance who preferred French cuisine or at least a Mediterranean fusion. She'd have his meal ready on his early nights, he'd eat, be gone. On late nights the pressure was off, but she'd prepare his meal, place it under plastic and reheat. She realized they never ate a meal together. She watched him, he never saw her. Eat. Saturdays were the same. And every second Sunday. The Sunday he had off, he'd spend catching up on reading research papers and writing for journals to ensure his professional development. Roger not only loved his work, he was driven by it. It made him, consumed him, empowered him. In their eight-year marriage, they'd gone on holiday once to Thailand. It wasn't what he preferred. He was a Francophile. As a student, he'd spent a year at

17

the Sorbonne in Paris; it had colored his world. Up every morning for study, then morning coffee (great coffee) at a sidewalk cafe with a croissant in his hand and an imaginary beret on his head. The baguette would come later. More study with students who knew their destiny, were not just in it for money or power or success. They loved medicine and all it entailed. Lunch was every day. Not just a sandwich in hand walking along to the next lecture. It was an event, a three-course feast with wine, and time. The French understood the art of enjoyment — food, wine and gifted conversation.

But Thailand was what Eve had organized. She'd asked him of course, had all the brochures, talked him into it. Said it would be relaxing, rejuvenating, a retreat. He didn't know what to do with himself. Couldn't sleep, found it too hot, didn't like swimming, couldn't find good coffee, the food was odd. Eve loved the intensity of the heat, the sudden rain squalls, the spicy cuisine. They stayed a week but he never left the hotel. They didn't travel again.

Eve's head started to throb with the familiar dull ache that reminded her of her dizziness earlier in the day. She held her hands to her head, closed her eyes and opened them again to see Roger standing in front of her in the kitchen. She stretched herself around his taut body. His arms did not return the warm pressure of a loving embrace.

'Hi babe, I felt so hot today. I think I may have a touch of heatstroke or something. I just came over all dizzy.'

'You often feel dizzy, Eve. I told you, you need more vitamins, building up. You don't have a strong constitution. You know you're supposed to be careful. You should take more care of yourself.' Eve brushed off the comments she had heard for the last two years.

Since it happened.

'How come you're home so early. What's up?' Eve looked at Roger who had now turned away.

'We need to have a chat about something.'

'What — I thought we'd sorted everything out — what now?'

Eve should have expected what came next. A marriage can't easily repair from third party interference. That was June. French, physician, same hospital, thrown together. Bound to happen. But he'd said it was over.

'Eve, I can't go on like this any more.' She pulled him closer at first as her tears melted into the front of his shirt causing a damp point around the third button. She could feel his heart beating fast. She moved away from the looseness in his hold.

'What is it — what do you mean?' Eve stood back a little so she could see his face.

'I'm leaving. I've got my bags ready. June is waiting. I'm sorry, Eve, but it's over. I can't look after you any more.' He looked over her head to the baggage in the doorway.

'But I thought we'd resolved this — I thought June was over. Don't leave now — I need you! I don't need looking after — I'm fine now. I'll be fine...'

'She's pregnant, Eve. You know it's what I want. There's not much more to discuss.' She saw the joy in his eyes when he told her, and remembered his look when she'd told him about their own baby.

She watched him pick up the bags, leave the keys in the tray by the door, give her a last look goodbye, the door close. Steps on the footpath, words at the gate. The car started and the engine growled as the car moved slowly away from the house.

4

E ve had barely slept and awoke with sore eyes and a painful back. When she finally opened her eyes, all she wanted to do was roll over and go back to sleep. She couldn't. Sleep had left her body and she had to face the day, one not like the day before. She made herself put on some clothes, went to the fridge and drank water to clear her head. She could tell the headache would come back again if not today, soon. Three days passed before she left the house, went to work, did some research, cooked. Or called her father.

After her three-day blackout, she remembered. Had to call him. At no answer a few times, she threw on some clothes and made herself presentable before driving over to see him. He had never allowed her to have a key, said it was not secure enough. It had irritated her at first but she had accepted this fact as one of his idiosyncrasies. She knocked on the front door, side door, windows — no response. She rang him from her mobile, still nothing. His car was there and she couldn't hear a sound. She waited and knocked again while the worst thoughts started to force their way into her head.

The police had to break a window and climb in. They found him in front of the mantelpiece curled up in a ball just as he had come into the world. He was still in his clothes — a cup, the tea long since evaporated, upended by his side.

As she stepped into the room, she sensed the worst had happened. He had died alone, the very circumstance he had always dreaded.

The policeman said he thought he was dead. Yet she could not feel sorrow. Her heart was pounding, her hands wet and her throat raspy. But her eyes were dry. It was only later when his body was gone and she was back in his house that she could let out the emotion. Opening the fridge she saw the food he had half eaten only days before, a loaf of bread with some slices gone, and half a tomato carefully wrapped in plastic film to delay the rot. In the midst of life. Her soul heaved and she couldn't stop the groans coming from her insides. It was as if a separate entity had taken hold of her. Her whole body racked itself until exhaustion. Eyes red and head pounding, she found herself on the lounge in front of the mantelpiece where her father had taken his last breath.

She thought of him curled up by the mantelpiece like a child just birthed from the womb. And helpless as a newborn, he had lost control of his body yet had no life left to feel embarrassment or indignation. His soul had left the remaining flesh alone.

She stood at the mantelpiece and thought of the many evenings warmed by the burning logs of the fireplace underneath. He had loved his open fires and continued them well into the warmer weather. He hadn't had a fire this season but the fragments of charcoal and dust remained. As she gazed at the open grate, her eye caught something in its peripheral vision. Pushed slightly under the grate of the fireplace was a small blue book, covered in dust.

Eve picked the book out of the ashes, trying not to coat her hands in grey dust. She sat on the sofa in the half light of afternoon thinking she knew her father, and arose knowing she did not. It appeared that the book was a diary written by someone from his past, a woman named Alexandra. She had written a letter to him asking him to go to Burma, she had something to tell him. The letter had been badly burnt. The book was more of a scrapbook, a collage of photos of a white-haired boy first in a black woman's arms, then being held by a young dark-haired woman. They were standing in front of a grand staircase of a large house, sprawling with a wide lawn and a courtyard in the front. There were drawings of hills, long boats and beaches, snippets of writing, and a few lines of verse most of which was not in English. She did not recognize the language. Although not all the sentences were connected, and she didn't recognize any names or people in the photos, she knew there was something in this diary that had tipped her father over the edge. It had been called a heart attack but she felt that it was a different type of attacker altogether.

It seemed there was much more to her father than she had ever imagined. She could see him in that young face now, the same piercing blue eyes, long nose and chin with the exaggerated ears he never liked. He was the white-haired boy with a childhood in Burma she knew nothing about, knowing people whose names were hard to spell and pronounce, in a house unknown to her. An intense sadness came over her as she remembered her father lying next to the fire, his trousers soiled. The tears came in an unending stream, flowing down her cheeks unchecked. She used to almost feel ashamed of his lack of self-importance, drive and ambition to do anything other than work nine to five, eat and sleep. That's what she believed he had always done. Now there was the possibility of something more, a life exotic and adventurous, in a faraway place she had never contemplated and knew little about.

The guidebooks and the Australian government said to avoid any country that was not a democracy. Yet this land was a link to her father's past — and consequently hers. Slowly, the idea emerged that she should travel to Burma herself, go in her father's place, find this woman and get the truth she claimed to have. There must be people alive who remembered him, the names in the diary would be a place to start. One name stood out — Dottmar Au-Yung. She didn't know how she would find this person, but she knew she had all the tools of the research trade at hand. She had nothing to hold her at home now.

She began to wonder what had been the truth he'd told her about her mother. He had told her she had died in an accident. He would never tell her details but she had assumed it had been a car accident. Her father had engendered a great and growing frustration in her with the way he would not tell the details of something as important as her mother's death. He became melancholy and said he didn't want to talk about it — it brought back too many painful memories. That may have been true at the time but it didn't stop Eve from asking probing questions for which she most often provided her own answers, as ludicrous as they may have seemed. Was he withholding about that too?

She could never again ask her father anything.

5

Eve had never thought of Burma as a travel destination. Reports in the news involved skirmishes and on newscasts the people appeared afraid and poor. The news item would last for three minutes and move onto the next hot spot in the world, a country's turmoil forgotten in an instant. All the travel agents said it was trouble. Not for holidays and not for tourists, she'd heard. She had travelled only to a couple of other cities in Australia — and once to Thailand. Beautiful Thailand that she'd loved. Burma was the last frontier even for intrepid travelers. Yet here she was on a plane ready to land in exotic Yangon which, she'd read, the locals still called Rangoon.

As the plane touched down on scorching tarmac, she reached inside her bag to look again at the black and white photo of a large colonial house surrounded by garden. She'd found this photo among her father's possessions. She hadn't liked fossicking through his things, felt it was disrespectful to his memory only two weeks after his funeral. But something drove her on. In between two birthday cards, she came across the photograph of a house. The best piece of luck was the handwritten address on the back of the photograph. Addressed to Dottmar Au Yung. Foreign sounding, obviously, but somehow strong. Man or woman?

She had handwritten a letter to Dottmar, feeling that the old-fashioned way was more polite. She explained who she was and that she wanted to meet. It had taken several weeks but she finally received a courteous response welcoming Eve to her home.

Airport security processing behind her, Eve walked out into the searing heat and was greeted by more people than she'd ever seen in one spot before. Faces pressed up against glass, against wire, against each other. Voices — loud, cacophonous, mesmerizing. The people were small and mostly dark. Their features, undifferentiated to her, merged into one until she could only see the crowd — not the people.

She forced her way through the mass of human life, trying to dodge the taxi hawkers and baggage handlers.

'Taxi, Miss,' called one. Then, another. And another.

'To the Yangon Hotel, please.' She would learn about bargaining later — now she just wanted to be in the nearest, coolest taxi — even if it did cost her three times local rates.

Eve had checked in, unpacked, showered and relaxed. She made her way to the lobby of the grand old Yangon Hotel where she had agreed to meet Dottmar, and watched the colorful catwalk in front of her. The residents of the hotel looked like tourists — pasty white faces and hands peeking out beneath long flowing shirts. They were over 55s mainly — bunched together like seagulls after chips. The noise outside was pretty much like seagulls too — the chirping and chattering hurt her ears. She couldn't blame them for that. She was getting used to the constant bleating of horns, hum and thump of traffic and perpetual noise of a mass of humanity — the yelling, chanting, offering, bargaining noises that are part of life in Asia.

Eve settled herself into a comfortable armchair and waited.

A figure emerged out of the mass — a figure with extended hands and a smile of unusually white teeth. Dottmar Au Yung was not young, and yet not old. Her hair was caught up in a bun of white — tamed by a bright blue bandana with curls escaping at the edges. As Eve stood, she realized Dottmar was about the same height as herself. Her dark eyes held Eve's stare as she introduced herself.

'Are you Eve?' Eve nodded. 'I knew it — you look like your father even though I have not seen him for so long!'

'Yes, Dottmar, is it? I'm glad you recognized me. How did you know who I was?'

'You can always spot an Australian, Eve, you must be aware of that!' she said smiling. 'It is the shoes that give you away.' Eve looked down at her flat sandals covering bare feet and wished she'd worn walking shoes like everyone else. But it was so hot — better to be an obvious tourist than have sweating feet.

'I am again so sorry about your dad...' Eve nodded.

Dottmar took hold of Eve's hand, guided her out of the hotel and into a waiting car. She moved swiftly, clutching the unruly gossamer fabric of her sari — the burgundies, reds and blues shimmering in the noon light.

'Eve, I know you've checked in here but I would like you to stay at my home. Would you?'

'What do you mean?'

'The family held on to the old home even after your father left for Australia. Did he not mention it? It belongs to him still.'

'No,' Eve said, wondering what else might have

been hidden from her.

'I will take you there now — then we can come back for your things. I hope you did not plan to stay long at the hotel!'

The streets of old Rangoon were alien to Eve. She'd seen documentaries on television but it was nothing like being there. The noise, the smells, the almost unbearable heat, heat that she thought she would love. Her hair went lank, her lightweight clothes stuck to her body, damp and uncomfortable.

'You will get used to it,' said Dottmar looking, to Eve, so clean and cool.

The taxi driver took several false turns down streets with no exit until under the tutelage of Dottmar, he managed to find himself on the right road. The car slowed in a street with few buildings — unlike the crowded and built up streets they had just passed. This street had many trees lining what could only be called a promenade. It had an old world charm about it — something Eve had not yet experienced in this ancient city. Finally, the taxi stopped outside a copse of large trees that obscured whatever residence lay behind. Dottmar spoke very fast to the driver, money was exchanged and she indicated to Eve to get out of the car.

Now she was standing in the street, Eve realized that the taxi had been relatively cool. The blistering sun was at its height. She stood near the trees which offered some shade and wondered how anyone could get used to this climate. Australia was hot but it didn't sap the energy like this.

'This way.' Eve followed Dottmar into the copse of trees which turned out to be the forecourt of a grand old home. It was built somewhere around the 1920s, Dottmar said. The forecourt opened out. She looked back and could see that the trees had been designed to form a barrier around the house — a natural wall to keep out prying eyes. She thought it was interesting that they had not just built a high stucco wall and been done with it. The trees were a nice addition, she thought.

As she made her way through the clearing and approached the house, she could see that it had once been glorious but had not had the human touch for a long time.

Up close, the house was tattered. The front door, though solid oak with a brass casing, would not close. So much for security, thought Eve. The window frames hung badly. She looked to the side of the house and saw other doors ajar. The driveway was overgrown with weeds — exotic ones she had never seen before. Among the tall, green stems of the mother weeds peeked their violet and yellow children covering the cement with a colorful carpet of life. She put her hands out to feel the coarseness of the cool sandstone columns by the front door. Paint peeled off in clumps as Eve ran her hands over the once-beloved walls.

'It needs a bit of work, doesn't it,' she said aloud.

'You should have seen it in our early years. It was a magnificent home to be around and grow up in. There were so many nooks and crannies for children to hide and play. It was perfect.'

Dottmar motioned Eve to follow her through the front door into the entry hall.

The red hallway carpet showed some signs of its former glory. The once-magnificent roses were faded into the beige of the underlay — never to flower again. The hallway blossomed into a bell-shaped room with the highest ceiling she had ever seen in a house. At the apex of the ceiling were stained glass windows depicting seraphim flying around the head of the Madonna. The faded red drapes hung unevenly around the room.

She appreciated the tatty grandeur of the place. It was old, unkempt and ignored. She hadn't been anywhere in the city, but driving past in the taxi she had noticed the other houses in the surrounding streets — their shiny balustrades, clean windows, and embroidered drapery at the windows. This house was different — it was the secret home of her father's childhood.

As they walked further into the house, Dottmar led her to a large door renovated with a new deadbolt system as its security. She pulled out the key and with some difficulty, unlocked the door.

'This is the main salon — we call it the Rose Room,' Dottmar said.

The room faced north and the first thing Eve noticed was that it was a huge open space, full of light originating from floor-to-ceiling windows protected by a large enclosed verandah. This room was different from the rest of the house. The windows were bare, the carpet ripped up to be replaced by brown natural fibred sisal. She had seen this material in sunrooms in Australia — it lasted for years. The odd thing about the room was that it was not furnished to be comfortable or to use in traditional Burmese style but was decorated like an office. There were many low desks with office chairs around the edge of the room. A few hat stands, some pots with plants in them (alive, she noticed), several computers on the desks and a phone next to every computer.

Eve turned to Dottmar with a questioning look to which the older woman raised her index finger to her mouth, grabbed Eve's hand and guided her to the verandah. Eve remembered the view from her own childhood home — high on a hill overlooking a shimmering river with the city in the background. It was spectacular. She looked out over the verandah railings now and took a deep breath. The house was built on the crest of a hill which fell away sharply to terraced layers of cultivated growth, then a transformation to wild forest. On either side were the protective twins of huge mountains covered in lush jungle which overshadowed the house. As far as the eye could see was a winding path of water — crashing against the rocky shore and softened by a white beach, a river falling away over the horizon under a bright blue sky.

She was about to turn to Dottmar again to exclaim in wonder, when she heard the door to the Rose Room close and footsteps approaching them on the verandah. Dottmar was facing the door when a man appeared.

'I would offer you both a drink but that wine collection has been gathering dust for 200 years and is now home to a veritable community of mice so you probably would refuse — and anyway, it is hardly drinking time yet. How about a Rangoon special?'

He gave Dottmar a hug, her eyes shone.

'Ko Tan, meet Eve from Australia.'

Eve looked at the figure who had just entered the room. He had bowed his head and taken her hand. He held it warmly with his two hands, bent down as if to kiss it but stopped midway. He looked up at her. His brown eyes were encircled by curled lashes. His face was strong and also brown, aged by the sun with deep lines at the corners of his eyes and around his mouth. She guessed his age to be close to Dottmar's — even similar to her father's — though he had the body of a young man. He was tall, with a broad upper body, greying hair worn long falling just under his ears. He wore the traditional *longyi* — pale blue western shirt worn over the sarong.

'I have heard a lot about you, Eve. I hope you will

be comfortable here. I am the caretaker of the house,' he added as Eve looked first at him, then at Dottmar.

'Hello. Thank you — um — this house, the room ... you're too kind,' said Eve.

Eve was attracted to younger men. She'd hated the way older men had babied her, tried to protect her. Younger men could be treated as equals. No pretenses. But this man was different. Even from this first meeting she was drawn to him, not attracted but there was something magnetic about his personality.

Her hand was still within his warm grasp, she realized it had been there too long. She withdrew it — his eyes did not leave her gaze.

'Eve, come and see your room.' Dottmar motioned them both to follow her through the Rose Room and again into the dark hallway. They turned and moved along to a locked door further down the corridor.

The door opened to reveal another expansive area bathed in light, which was prepared for a visitor. Antique furniture filled the room — a carved bed adorned with what Eve assumed was a local Burmese silk bed covering. A marriage chest nestled in the corner, and a massive ancient wardrobe festooned with colorful tassels sat beside it. Double ornate doors opened onto the balcony — home to a wrought iron table and chair overlooking the same vista as the Rose Room — mountains, jungle and river.

Handmade silk rugs of dazzling colors dotted the polished wooden floor — one large rug covered most of the floor space and two smaller ones lay on either side of the bed.

'Do you like it, Eve?' Dottmar smiled, waiting for a response.

'Dottmar, it's magnificent. Are you sure it's OK that I stay here?'

'Of course — you must stay — as long as you like.'

'Can you tell me one thing — what is that room used for — the Rose Room. People obviously work in there. What's going on?'

She saw a flicker in Dottmar's eye. 'Do not worry about that for now. We will tell you tomorrow. Settle in and I will come and get you for dinner at 6.'

Eve slumped on the bed to discover magical comfort, awakening a couple of hours later to the sound of tapping at the door. She roused herself and padded across the room.

A young Burmese girl was at the door, holding what looked like colorful garments. The girl bowed to Eve, her eyes downcast.

'Ma'am — some clothes for you tonight, and items for your bath.'

'Thank you. What's your name?'

'Mya.'

'Do you live here too?'

'Yes I work for Ko Tan — in the house.'

The girl spoke quietly and Eve felt that was about as much information she would get from her — for now.

As she took the bundle of garments from Mya, Eve looked at her and smiled. She noticed something glitter around her neck.

'That's a lovely pendant.' The girl looked up instantly as her hand clasped the piece. She then softened, and held it in front of Eve's face. It was one half of a silver coin.

'It's unusual,' Eve said. 'Why is there only half a coin?' The girl stepped back as the pendant fell out of Eve's fingers and settled back at the girl's neck.

'I will take you to the dining room — I wait outside while you dress.'

Even though Eve thought the girl was strange, she

realized she had a lot to learn about the culture and the people. She took the clothes and a small package from Mya before the girl closed the door to wait outside. The traditional female sarong was sky-blue and edged with gold embroidery; the top was a shortened bodice, matching the sarong's color with long sleeves. She wondered about the wisdom of so much material in the heat of the day. For now, though, she was sick of her tourist clothes and longed for a shower. She looked around and saw a door which, earlier, she had taken for a closet. The large, carved wooden structure gave way with a light push and opened onto a bathroom. The bath was set into the floor, three steps leading down to it. On the opposite side was a large bath. The room appeared to be constructed from marble — mottled pink and grey and, from a huge picture window, offered the same majestic view as the small balcony. Eve marveled at the mix of traditional and modern in the room's design which, she guessed, would not be an inexpensive exercise. She started the bath which filled quickly as she peeled off her sweat-dampened clothes. She immersed herself in the steamy water and, remembering the small package Mya had given her, reached around. It was a jar of aromatic bath powder. Eve rarely indulged herself in luxuries. She felt guilty for a moment before she let the aroma and heat take her to another place.

'Eve — you look stunning.'

After patiently waiting, Mya had escorted Eve to the dining room as she had promised, where Eve noticed Ko Tan looking at her. She had tried to get the sarong to wind around her body as she had noticed Dottmar's do. She hoped the effect had worked.

'The blue is reflected in your eyes — exquisite,' Ko Tan said.

Eve blushed again, hating that she could never hide

her embarrassment. She wondered how often he used that line. She turned to see Dottmar already seated, gesturing her to sit next to her.

'Eve, I hope you do not mind, but we have asked two others to join us later this evening. Among other things, they work for us. Do not worry, you will like them.'

Eve usually felt shy and awkward meeting people for the first time. She was stretching her boundaries and felt it.

'Who are they?' she asked.

'They will join us after entrée.'

At precisely the end of entrée, Dottmar rose to greet two men, roughly Eve's age. Both bore a striking resemblance to Ko Tan.

'Meet my sons, Than and Abau. This is Eve — our house guest from Australia.'

They smiled broadly at Eve who smiled awkwardly in return. They said little at dinner which she took to mean they spoke little English. What they did say was privy only to themselves in muted conversations between courses. Mya, who now appeared to be both chef and waitress for the evening, was not included in the sit down guest list. Whenever she entered the room, both Than and Abau would stop murmuring and watch as she set the dishes before retreating to the kitchen, followed by a snicker between themselves.

'What do you both do for your father?' They had neither asked about her nor volunteered any information about themselves. Eve was curious. They glanced at their father before Than spoke. Eve guessed he was the older of the two.

'We work as administrative assistants while on our study leave. We are both studying at Yangon University — accounting.'

This seemed to amuse Abau as Eve struggled to imagine these two exotic young men as accountants. But, most people never would have thought she had a doctorate in horticulture.

'Oh, do you find it interesting?'

They exchanged glances before looking to their father who answered for them.

'It is late. Abau and Than have work to do. We need to adjourn to the library. Come.'

Ko Tan led the young men from the table through a hall toward another room which Eve guessed was the library.

Dottmar said, 'Eve, you must stay tonight and tomorrow we will pick up your things and check you out of the hotel.' Eve assumed she would be shown into the library to enjoy after-dinner cognac with the men — or whatever men did in libraries. She was mistaken.

'Mya will see you to your room.' Dottmar turned and walked from her toward the other end of the house.

Mya appeared from the kitchen, wiping her hands before removing her apron.

'It's alright, Mya. I can manage. Good night.'

The constant escorting and formalities were starting to irritate Eve. She made her way to the hallway which led to her room. To her right was the library door which was slightly ajar.

She stopped, hearing only muffled sounds as she leant her head towards the wood paneling. She heard someone talking, then a squelching sound, some curious beeps, and then another even more muffled voice. A pause, then louder words. The words were difficult to understand. Ko Tan's voice was the loudest but what she heard made no sense.

She heard her name and then 'Alex'. The voice was clear now, Ko Tan must be close to the door. She wasn't quick enough, having only time to face the corridor before Ko Tan appeared in the open doorway. He looked her straight in the eyes.

'If you wanted an after-dinner drink, you should have said. We are just not used to ladies wanting to join us. Come in.'

'Dottmar said to go to bed so I ...'

'Dottmar does not drink and I am sure you do,' Ko Tan took her hand with a firm grip and guided her into the library.

'The boys are leaving so it will be just you and me. I hope you do not mind?' Than and Abau moved around her to leave the room. Both stared at her as they left.

'No, of course not. They're not really boys, though. Aren't they about my age?' Not that she was going to admit what that was.

'They will always be my boys. They have been through a lot with me as their father.' Ko Tan moved to a drinks cabinet, gestured to a bottle filled with bubbly clear liquid.

'Champagne?'

'You're not the caretaker, are you Ko Tan? And I'm curious to know what this house is used for.'

'Oh, later. Take this and we will talk.'

Ko Tan had learnt English, he told her, at the international school before later studying international politics and philosophy at the same university where his sons now studied.

'Politics and philosophy. What made you choose that pair of subjects?'

'You ask a lot of questions for a doctor of horticulture.'

'How did you know that?'

'I research everyone who is a guest in my house.' He took a sip from his crystal glass and placed it on the low oak table between them.

'Dottmar told me this was my father's house and still is. Did you know my father? What was he like? Did you know my mother too?'

'One thing at a time. First, I want to show you something.'

He stood and moved around to the drawers on his desk, opened one and took out an envelope. Returning, he proffered it to Eve. She reached inside and pulled out a photograph.

The picture was old and partly yellowed. It showed a class of very young children obediently sitting in a row of chairs with their hands on their knees. The plaque at their feet said: 'Rangoon School — Class of 1948'.

Eve peered at the dark-haired, dark-eyed children in the picture. One child stood out. He had white blond hair, blue eyes and pale white skin. With his two friends on either side of him, the boy was unable to hide his infectious grin. Eve could see they were the boy's friends as they were looking in his direction and smiling. The three personalities shone like a beacon in the photograph, revealing a deep bond. A blond boy, a dark-haired girl, and a coal-faced boy.

'Are you implying that this is my father? With you and Dottmar?'

'You are a smart woman, Eve. I knew you would learn very fast. I am not implying anything. It is a fact.'

The three children had met on the first day of school, Ko Tan told Eve. Alex was from a wealthy family of expatriates, originally the descendants of a missionary who had settled in Burma. The family and its offspring had stayed ever since, and Alex had merged with the locals at the school as if he had been one of them.

Ko Tan could remember that first day when

Dottmar, his babyhood friend and neighbor had been transfixed by the flaxen-haired boy, hair color she had never seen before. She had reached out to touch it and Alex had swung around in a flash, frightening the young girl into a corner. She had stayed there all day, too afraid to come out. The two boys had secretly laughed about this, instantly forming a friendship. Dottmar had brought them together. They would not know for a long time that she would also break them apart.

All three were the brightest in their year — their natural intelligence complemented by enquiring minds. They learned the history and geography of their beloved but beleaguered land and, in doing so, developed a passion for their country and the rights of its people.

'Dottmar loved your father from the first moment she saw him. He saw her only as a friend … in the same way he saw me as a friend. She always wanted more from him. But he never loved her the way I loved her.'

Ko Tan lowered his head and his shoulders began to shake. He covered his eyes with his hands. Eve put her hand on his heaving shoulder.

'That must have been hard for you.' She wasn't sure what else to say. Rarely did she find herself being a counsellor and she didn't like it. She didn't allow herself to get close enough to people to offer advice.

'It has been hard for me. I have always loved her.'

'But you're together now, aren't you?' Eve seized on the chance to satisfy her curiosity while giving what she considered a sensitive response.

Having calmed himself for a few moments, Ko Tan's shoulders once more began to shake. He removed his hands from his eyes which Eve was shocked to see were shining and dry. Clearly, his shoulders had been heaving not from sorrow but from laughter.

'Together — now — ha!'

Ko Tan picked up his glass, skulled the remaining fluid and plonked the vessel loudly on the table. 'We must close the library now and get some sleep. I will talk to you tomorrow. Good night.'

'But Ko Tan — are you OK? Why are you laughing like that?'

He closed his mouth and put his glass down. 'It is difficult for someone like you to know. In this country, friendships are not always what they seem, motives are often changing. Best that you just observe and learn. When the time comes, you will know.'

'I need to show you something too. It's why I'm here.' She pulled the diary from her bag and handed it to Ko Tan. As he looked at the pages, his face remained unchanged.

'This is written by Alexandra, your grandmother. It was she who asked your father to come back. Unfortunately, Eve, you are too late. She died only weeks ago — from cancer.'

'Oh no — I so much wanted to meet her, Ko Tan. She would have had so much to tell me. Did you know her well?'

'No — not well. She had left by the time I met Alex, many years before. I know nothing about her. The news of her death has reached me by our communications network. She was involved also in the government. But enough — I need to sleep.' He passed the diary back to her.

She wanted to ask him more questions but saw that the mood had changed and he was ready for sleep.

'Alright Ko Tan. Good night. I hope we can talk more another time.'

She followed him from the library to find Mya waiting in the hallway — for her or Ko Tan she couldn't say. Eve nodded her good night as Mya slipped into the library to tidy the glasses and drinks cabinet. Ko Tan was striding toward what she supposed was his bedroom. He didn't look back.

Eve made her way through the corridors to her room where, after closing the bedroom door, she opened the curtains and doors to the balcony. The warm, richly scented night air greeted her — something she had not experienced before — and as she wallowed in its warmth, she heard the sounds of people in the valley far away and of bird life in the jungle. The night was abuzz, with every sound magnified but soon the birds' calls began to sound eerie. She turned back to the bedroom and prepared for bed, where comfort enveloped her for another eight hours.

*

The sun burned through the lightness of the curtains and she was surprised how early the heat of the day had started.

She felt well rested, eager to bathe and dress and get back to the hotel. Hospitality can go so far, she thought. It was time to be independent again, although both Ko Tan and Dottmar needed to provide some answers. After bathing she dressed in her tourist clothes with the inappropriate sandals of the previous day. She noticed the house had a different feel to it today. As she made her way around the hallway and into the main salon, she realized that nobody had shown her where the kitchen was. She needed coffee. She heard noises in the Rose Room and opened the unlocked door.

Every desk housed a computer, phone/fax and radio and on every chair at every desk was a person — all young, a few males but mostly females. Every desk was piled with paper, both on the desktop and all over the floor space below. She turned to her left and saw, sitting at a grand desk with a leather wing back chair, Than, Ko Tan's eldest son. He appeared agitated barking orders into a hand-held radio in what, from her little knowledge of the language, she supposed was Burmese. A squelching noise emanated from the radio, then silence. Than looked up scowling and saw her. His face drained of color as he rose from his chair.

'You cannot be in here. Please go.'

'What's going on?' she asked with more confidence than she felt.

'It's no business of yours — now go.' About to retort she felt a soft pressure on her arm.

'Eve, come and have breakfast. We want to talk to you.'

She followed Dottmar to yet another room, this one leading out onto the courtyard decorated with colorful pots, three chairs and a wrought iron table. Ko Tan was already seated, Mya was pouring tea.

'Good morning, Eve. Come and join us for an English breakfast.'

'Look, I'm not very hungry. I just need to know what's going on.' She felt insolent and provocative but most of all angry.

'You have stumbled upon our Headquarters, Eve. The beating heart of our party. I know you have many questions. Your father worked for the party; his father before him was one of its founders. That is how we were able to take over the house for our own use. With your father's blessing.'

'What sort of party?'

'Freedom, Eve. Freedom from the subjugation of our citizens. Freedom for us all. We are working hard to free Burma!'

'So you're with the Democratic Party?'

'We are all working to free not just the Burmese

people, but all minority groups in this once-great country. But it is not easy. We have enemies all around us. It is difficult to know who we can trust. Everyone works for someone. We have to stay on our guard.'

'Why did you ask me to the house? Did you want me to find out even though it seems a secret?'

Dottmar who had been standing by her side spoke. 'Eve, your father left Burma because of the violence. He found out it was not going to be a peaceful mission when two forces want their own set of opposing goals. He saw many die. Some very close to him. In the end, he fled from his beloved Burma, fled from his duty and responsibility. He failed us. But we have confidence that you will not.'

Eve was beginning to create an image of the father she had never known. From her knowledge of him being a quiet, unambitious, solitary and homely man, she had instantly magnified his image into that of a landowner, founder of civil rights for the common people, fighter for freedom. A beautiful woman had loved him her whole life. Now this image was disintegrating before her eyes. Her father had become ordinary again. Her shoulders sagged, the light in her eyes was gone.

'The man you knew and loved for so many years was disloyal?' Eve said looking at Dottmar.

Dottmar threw a glance at Ko Tan, her eyes black. She looked at Eve, her expression softening.

'We cannot blame him for that. In those early days he had such grand ideas. But they were difficult to implement. The forces were too strong for him. He lost his spirit. Australia beckoned and one day he just left.'

Eve could not believe this of Alex. Even though in her lifetime he had not achieved what she might call greatness, she could never think of him as a coward.

'We want you to come and work for us, Eve. In the

party.' Ko Tan focused on her eyes as he spoke.

Eve's first reaction was to laugh. She wondered what skills they thought she had that could help them free a population under such rigid control.

'That's ridiculous. For one thing I can't stay here legally; and for another I have a job at home. And what would I do anyway? How on earth could I help?'

'We can organize working visas legally, you have no ties at home — we know that. You will be our resident scientist.'

'How can you organize ... how do you know about my ties ... resident scientist? What does that mean? I'm a horticulturalist, not a spy!'

'Oh Eve, you have been watching too much television! We have many ideas about how we can use your skills. Why not at least think about it, try it out for a couple of weeks and if it does not suit you, you can go home. We will pay for your travel and expenses, and you can live here. Give it a try.'

Privately, she had to admit to herself that the old woman's garden didn't sound nearly as exciting as being the scientist-in-chief of the freedom party of Burma. Were they right? There was nothing much to go back to. Could she give it two weeks?

'Only if I can find out more about my father's life. I'll stay the two weeks here and decide.'

6

Mandalay, the second largest city in Burma, was once a great metropolis; plundered, beaten and passed around among the supreme deities of the western world. Having gained independence all those years ago, the city survived. Its current state was inglorious yet robust — perhaps even strong enough to build a dream for the small community which still inhabited the great delta of the river or the jungles of the high country. As most had fled the streets of the fallen city, now once more in the hands of renegade trustees, many made their way to the sanctuary of the high country.

One such family, Chau Lap, had survived. Despite hardship, they had been able to settle in a clearing which would become the community known as Praya. Others joined them where they existed on the fruits of their beloved land. The fruits were in demand by groups who found their way to Praya. Their crops were not fruits, but seeds that grew from the magnificent yellows and reds of the soft flower with the long furry stem known as the poppy. It was the seeds inside the petals that were harvested and were now fetching large sums of money. Mama and Papa Chau-Lap had not asked what they were used for, nor questioned why they were so eagerly acquired. All they knew was they could feed their family.

As a child, Papa Chau-Lap had been able to help his father farm the land, the soldiers had not interfered. As Papa had grown and created his own family, times had changed. The rebels could no longer be ignored and, in order to sustain their food supplies, the precious poppy was the only plant that was allowed to be harvested. What they were promised they received and the harvest was bountiful — he was well rewarded. Life could have carried on in this way if only democracy had not stepped in.

The democratic government was instituting regular slash and burn expeditions to counter Western criticism of what they considered nefarious activities on the border. For Papa Chau-Lap, life had become a game of hit and run, a dangerous game that put his family and community at risk.

One morning before dawn, the skies watching over his developing crop burst into a wondrous display of oranges, reds and yellows and with the colors, a heat of such intensity that the birds flew in all directions to escape its clasp. The soldiers stood at the side of the field, their fire-breathing metal dragons holding no sympathy. The flamethrowers desecrated the landscape in front of his eyes.

He gathered his family and a few belongings as he watched his home go up in flames, and began the long walk to the next village where he would plant the seeds for another crop of poppies. To begin again would cost everything he had saved. This was the pattern of each hill dweller's existence.

*

One son from another Mandalay family, Josefo, had never returned to that city from his new mountain home. Having abandoned his childhood life, he was now able to travel freely on his own business and that of his leader. He often travelled to the south to gather information and to pass on intelligence from the mountains.

This lost son was making one of his regular trips to Rangoon. He found himself in the Central Market at the end of a busy Saturday. The market stall holders were setting up for the evening session amid the cries of street sellers, hawkers, barking dogs, crying children and the click clack of mahjong tiles between geriatric fingers. The young man wasn't fooled. Behind dilapidated curtains in two-room dwellings, those fingers gambled thousands of Kyat in one night.

'Josefo! I have some fantastic durians for you to try!' yelled one stall holder.

'You can keep your durians,' Josefo called back. 'But I will have a bag of your juiciest papaya.'

It was the fruit of his childhood in Mandalay. Josefo enjoyed reminiscing about his past — he loved the sounds, sights, smells of the city he didn't know well but he always managed to eat the fruit, drink the juice and smell the fragrances that took him back to a time of peace — one that his senses could remember though his mind could not.

He would spend hours strolling through the crowds, testing the samples, stealing a paw paw here, a copy watch there, never having to exchange the crass Kyat currency to survive but always gaining the precious American note. Josefo had an unusual talent. Often he thought about where he might have learned this talent, though his mind did not dwell on the problem long enough to solve it. Yet the talent, which, in another time may have been called trickery, or even thievery, remained. Josefo preferred to think of himself as an entrepreneur.

As Josefo strolled through the crowd, his casual stride belied his intense interest in everything around him, his eyes darting to and from every corner. He did not walk in a straight line but veered side to side, all the while watching the arc to his right and left, ever vigilant of his surroundings and the activities of others around him. He had grown up in the jungle. Perhaps the Burmese tiger had always been near — he sensed it now and was ever-watchful. He was looking for something in particular.

He smiled and the young town girls threw him admiring glances — a smile like that on a boy from outside the city. What a treat! His arms and shoulders were strong and his height was more than the average Rangoon man.

Josefo needed to focus. He had enjoyed his time strolling through the evening market drinking in the warm night. He had a duty to perform. He remembered his instructions: shop for supplies, rendezvous with the target and return to camp.

'We know that the granddaughter of the Tiger is presently in Rangoon. I want to meet this woman and find out what she knows. Also find her father. He has a debt to pay. If she is in Burma, she knows something,' San Wu said.

His leader, San Wu, had passed instructions to Josefo. It was a major test for Josefo to prove himself and move forward in the ranks. He had been patient long enough. There were few chances for promotion so he must do what San Wu asked regardless of the danger. He hadn't minded — he had personal business in

Rangoon so it wouldn't be too much out of his way. The intelligence about the female was that she may be in danger — what that meant he didn't know. His orders were to travel to the main square just before midnight and if she hadn't materialized, he was to pay a visit to the grand old house. He would figure out the next steps later.

He reached into his pocket and pulled out the tattered photographic paper. She had a certain appeal. He hadn't met many western women, most were too pasty for him but he could see the attraction. She had a warmth, even with the unruly hair and spectacles — the learned type. A strong face with a small nose and freckles. Could be a problem. He doubted there would be any trouble finding her. The problems would come later.

He had one other contact to meet before midnight.

7

Eve had become used to the corridors leading to wide parlors, the staircases and silk rugs. Dottmar had shown her a few of the sights of the city once called the Paris of the East, and insisted she visit the magnificent Shwedagon Temple, an imposing golden presence in the middle of the city. Eve could find her way back to the house and into the main square easily. Mostly she walked but sometimes the heat became unbearable, so she preferred the air-conditioned taxis that prowled the streets for clients.

The heat concerned her at first. This had been the trigger two years ago. It was probably unrelated but she kept her pills close at all times and never skipped. They had kept her together and she intended to stay that way. It was the same the day she fainted in the old woman's garden. Don't let go, and she would stay constant. It was June's fault really. Nothing to do with Roger. He was just caught up in the excitement of it, a new woman showing affection he couldn't resist. The French connection. He'd come back to her, had still loved her. June was over. But Eve became something she could not describe. An unbelievable sadness she never would have thought possible, a physical bereavement yet no one had died. Her body was racked with sickness she could not shake. But the sickness was in her mind, not her blood and flesh. He had seen that and been back to cure her of the sickness he had caused, they had caused.

It seemed a long time ago yet it was merely weeks. The next time. The last time. She knew it would happen. Tried to keep the tide back in the path of a cyclone. June had won. France had beaten Australia. If she hadn't cried all those nights, hadn't sobbed, begged him to come back, promised to give him what he wanted, the baby. He would have stayed. She thought. But he could not forget what she had done.

The memory of that time of her life came in and out, floating between images of her father, of them eating together, chatting, of his body by the fireplace, of his young child's face, the blond hair she had never seen before. Being in such a foreign place was still part of that dream. Somehow, she could not believe that she had travelled to Burma. She wanted to find out about her father's past. Why had it taken her so long, now when she could not ask him, speak to him, share anything with him again. Could she also find out about her mother?

She was walking back into the courtyard when she spotted one of the brothers watching her from a window on the second storey. As she drew closer, she saw it was Abau. He didn't hide the fact that he was staring at her. Most people when discovered peeping, would close the curtains, pretend it hadn't happened. But he stood and watched as she walked up to the front door and passed through. He didn't smile or blink. Eve waved at him, but he gave no response. She found him unlikeable and decided to avoid him. The older brother wasn't much friendlier but at least he stayed away from her and appeared to have no interest. That's how she liked it.

Ko Tan was an enigma like much she had found in

this country. His presence had caused an unlikely reaction in her which she now realized was nothing to do with her. He was a performer, a trickster — Shakespeare would have called him a dissembler. It was attractive at first, but she felt he had a dark side she was not willing to probe too deeply.

It had been two weeks and if she decided to stay, she would have to start looking at embassies and paperwork. The initial excitement Dottmar and Ko Tan had stirred in her to work in the party had subsided. The only working she had done was some filing at the end of the day when the Rose Room was empty of workers. Dottmar had asked her to collect all the papers on all the desks and sort them by memo number into filing cabinets at the corner of the room. She had not gathered any information this way as the memos were not in English, so had to be filed numerically. By the end of the week, she had not had any further library chats with Ko Tan and any information she felt she might get at the beginning of the trip had diminished to nothing. She had shown Dottmar the diary, but she'd seemed unable or unwilling to provide any further clarification about the photographs or what Alexandra may have been waiting to tell Alex.

'I'm leaving tomorrow, Dottmar. I don't think there's much I can do here and I don't want the hassle of changing my visa stuff.' Dottmar's face went pale.

'If that is the way you feel, Eve, but we were just starting to get to know each other! I will miss you!' Dottmar reached out her hand and touched Eve's. Eve's face went red again and she looked down

'The plane leaves tomorrow night. I'll pick up some things from the hotel and then head to the airport from. You've been fantastic, Dottmar, thank you so much.'

They hugged and Eve was the first to pull away.

8

Ever since being in this country, Eve had had a rasping thirst. She'd experienced this in the bush during her training in outback Western Australia. There the sun was relentless, drying, disintegrating moisture on any surface. Here was different — it was hot but the wetness of everything made the heat stick to your insides. There was no escape from that sickly, trickling heat. Eve preferred the dryness of her homeland, even with the skin cancer epidemic.

Eve remembered the conversation with Ko Tan and Dottmar. There was something that she couldn't explain — gut instinct perhaps. The feeling that they knew something but weren't willing to tell her. Perhaps she was not meant to know. She'd found out more than she had imagined. Maybe that was enough. She started packing her clothes. She had changed out of her *longyi* and was back in the khaki shorts and sandals of her first day. She maneuvered her case from within the wardrobe and placed that too on the bed so that she could see what would fit. Eve was not fond of shopping and had bought only a few trinkets from the marketplace stalls one afternoon. Her bag was no heavier than it had been when she arrived. Toiletries were the last to go in. She checked again — money, passport, ticket.

Her dry mouth was crying out for water.

As she walked into the bathroom, she heard a tap on the door. It was late, she had said her goodbyes earlier in the day. Ko Tan had been charming, had shown no sign of distress. Dottmar said again she would miss Eve. She had thanked them for their kind hospitality. The maid girl would not knock on her door. She had made herself scarce and Eve rarely saw her around the house. Returning from the bathroom, she opened the door and saw a disheveled young man, dark and brooding.

'Abau, it's a bit late to be knocking on my door, don't you think?' He stood in the doorway not steady on his feet. His eyes opened and closed more quickly than normal but there was intensity in those black eyes she did not like.

He pushed the door wide and lunged into the room. Eve nearly fell over her feet but managed to stay upright. He was a big man, slow but strong. He grabbed her neck and pushed her back towards the bed. His grip was tight, she could barely breathe and couldn't scream.

He didn't say a word. He stuffed something in her mouth and covered it with sticking tape. The taste was minty but the gag almost made Eve vomit. She had no way of making a noise. He managed to get her arms behind her back and tie them with some rough rope. Should she kick, head butt — she couldn't scream or move. He placed her shoulder bag and suitcase over one shoulder and with the other arm pulled her off the bed and moved toward the door. He forced her down the corridor and into a side bedroom. It was small containing one single bed and a wardrobe. He threw the case and bag into the wardrobe, locked it and pocketed the key.

Now with two arms, he closed the door and headed toward the main entrance through the front door, and across the courtyard. Hardly able to walk to keep up with the towering man, Eve dragged her feet as he pulled her out into the night.

9

M ya was alone in the kitchen when she saw Abau and the white woman moving past the bushes outside the house. She could see Abau's distinctive large shape plodding through the garden heading toward the village covering the smaller figure with his arm. The head of the taller figure kept turning to look behind and Mya was certain he looked straight into the light of the kitchen window.

She darted to the light switch, killed the light and moved slowly back to the window. As her eyes adjusted to the darkness, she could see only the woman's feet being dragged along in sandals. She wondered for a brief moment if this was another of Abau's little games to get her back into his bed. Make her think he had someone else and she would come running back. On second look, Mya could see that the woman was not accompanying Abau of her own free will. Her head was covered with a hood. She knew Abau had unusual hobbies which involved mostly evening activities but what could he be up to with the Australian woman? She knew also that he was not partial to the white variety. Mya would be patient — news from the village would soon filter to her. She may be able to use his bumbling action to her advantage.

Abau's games had worked for a while, she had to admit, and he had served his purpose. But she had a larger target in her sights. Ko Tan was the one she wanted, not because he loved and cared for her — though he had been gentler with her than most others. He was the leader and she needed him.

She had used all men, Abau and Than in their turn. But she was done with them, having received nothing more than a few trinkets. Her desires had grown beyond material things. As she watched the two figures disappear into the night, she remembered fragments of a similar event; the event she had tried hard to forget, but never her brother. She wanted her memories to begin when she had first seen Ko Tan.

*

As a 14-year-old girl with dark eyes, unkempt hair and someone else's clothes, she had been offered to him by the traders dealing in servants.

Ko Tan had needed a housekeeper. The party was growing daily, members were joining and there were more people in the house on the day shift than ever before. The cook couldn't cope. Ko Tan didn't like the concept of the sale of human beings but it was the only way he could get reliable servants at reasonable rates. He had a household to run.

'She is a bit young,' he had said at the time.

'None of them are young. You will find she will do.'

After negotiation, he had passed over some cash. 'Does she have any bags or possessions to bring in?'

'Just what you see.'

'What is your name, girl?' Ko Tan sensed what he first thought was fear in her eyes. Later he realized it was anger, the kind of anger that doesn't go away.

'My name is Mya. I am pleased to be here, sir,' her

smile instantly overshadowed the anger Ko Tan had thought he'd witnessed. It was certainly a beguiling smile — one he wasn't aware she had practiced for such an occasion. He had to admit he was charmed. She looked as if she knew how to trade with men.

He had taken her on, paid for her expenses in exchange for housekeeping. She was a willing and hard worker. It astounded her that this was all he wanted. And it would have continued.

It was she who offered Ko Tan more than just dusting the shelves, washing dishes and ironing clothes. And that did not include cooking. She could see he was appalled. She was only a child and he was married to a woman he had loved forever. But Dottmar had become distracted with her position in the party and had neglected his pampering. Mya offered herself and wanted nothing in return.

He was flattered — an older man such as he seduced by a young girl his granddaughter's age — if he'd had one. It had been easy with older men — men who had only loved one woman were a different kind from those she was used to. Gentle, loving and unselfish were words she was not familiar with. She had grown a genuine kind of love for him — a slow and comfortable love that made her feel secure, safe, in the middle of his heart and home. Having experienced this love of sorts, she knew she could never lose it. She had found her resting place and she would secure it. If her brother was alive, she would find him, let him know she had survived — more than survived — prospered under circumstances she could not and would not speak of to another. But those circumstances would never befall her again.

The experiment with Abau had happened before Ko Tan. She had thought he had more power in the party so being with him could have been strategic. But once she realized that the father was the leader, Abau had to go. It wasn't so hard — plant the seed and the crop grows.

What did Abau want with that white woman? And why had she come here? Burma didn't need whites like her — it could survive on its own. The kidnappings and drugs could only stop when Western influences were no longer of importance to the government. That was the problem — not the country.

She was standing at the sink when she noticed her hands starting to shake. She gripped the metal edge as tightly as she could to stabilize the flesh that would soon be uncontrollable. Ko Tan had guessed what her needs were early on even though he had tried to ignore her changing moods and strange habits. It was only from that first night together when he saw the physical signs from her past which had become her constant companion.

She walked down the corridors to her part of the house — the small servant's bedroom next door to Ko Tan's study. It held nothing more than a bed and clothes rack. When the door had closed, she reached under the bed and pulled out a wooden box, well worn with the former polish almost rubbed off.

The syringe beckoned. Her heart beat faster in anticipation of the pleasure; her mouth went dry.

She reached into the old wooden box. It held a ball of black tar-like matter within a plastic wrapper, a syringe, matches, a piece of plastic cord, and a spoon. She had been saving the black-tar variety for something special. It was no longer so accessible, the white powder had become easier to get. She avoided the more difficult score. She didn't often use the syringe, this would be the last time with the black-tar. She decided inhaling was less messy, quicker but had the same result.

She took the plastic ball, unwrapped the black pasty matter and put the whole ball onto the spoon. It was a larger spoon which would be needed to meld the matter into liquid for her waiting vein. She lit a match and held it under the spoon for what seemed an eternity. She would need to light several matches to dissolve this quality of black-tar.

After preparing her vein for its visitor, she fed the syringe with the brown liquid.

The cold thin steel entered her supple skin and pulsed its bountiful fruit throughout her veins and into her system. Instantly her skin flushed and her legs and arms felt heavy as weights. The rush was exhilarating and this time, a dry mouth was her only discomfort. She had become used to that. Sometimes, she would feel nauseous and vomit. Then the itching started. She hated that. But for now, it was intense. This batch would keep her going for a few hours, maybe a couple of days. She would be satisfied for a while until she needed it the next time, and the next, and the next ...

Her vision faded to a dream as sleep overcame her.

10

J osefo meandered through the broken slabs of concrete and weeds growing out of the cement. He knew the streets of Rangoon well but even he could get confused. One lane merged into another and all the doorways looked alike. He found his way down one, looked up and saw a grand old building in the middle of a plaza. It was to be a standard switch he'd accomplished many times before with the same brothers but they never came together. It was always one or the other. If the worst happened, they couldn't risk losing both. This time was nothing unusual, he just had to rendezvous, pass over the stash, get the money and walk. One-on-one. A five-minute job — one of the easiest. As he approached from the side, behind the large building off the plaza, he saw two figures approaching him in the dark.

The brothers must have come together, he thought. It was not wise, but sometimes necessary. If they thought there was a high level of risk to one, the other would hide in the shadows preparing for attack. He wondered why they would have thought he was a threat. One appeared to be shorter than the other in the shadows. Josefo's eyes swiveled, noting his arc of protection as he slowly neared the couple cloaked in darkness.

The figures held back in the shadows until he had also been enveloped by darkness.

'Where is it?' said the familiar voice.

Josefo was weary of distrust. 'Here as always, my friends. I see you both have come — do you not trust the faithful Josefo?' He handed over his parcel, receiving in return an envelope which he opened, checked and saw was empty. He looked up at the two figures and noticed the shorter figure squirm. He realized it was not the two brothers. There was a stranger in his midst.

'Where is my money? Who have you brought here? You do not bring strangers when we deal.'

The shorter figure was huddled behind the larger one, looking uncomfortable in the blackness. The larger figure pulled the smaller figure in between them. Abau's face now showed in the moonlight. He was struggling with the smaller figure which he pushed forward. At the same time, he shoved a piece of shiny paper into Josefo's hand.

'Tell San Wu she is his for 50 grand — American money. Consider the money from the envelope your deposit — already paid.' Josefo looked at the paper in his hands. It was a picture of a woman. She had blondish hair, spectacles, eyes lowered to the ground — not a local. It was very similar to the photo he had in his pocket.

The struggling figure murmured then emerged into the moonlight. It was the same woman. Her mouth was gagged, and it appeared her hands were bound. Her eyes were not frightened but showed a determination that reminded Josefo of someone. So this was the woman San Wu, his great leader, knew was in the country and wanted to meet. And she had landed right in his lap. What a coup! An easy night's work. The only thing now was whether to appear that he knew she was valuable or to make out that she was worth nothing. And he wanted his money. Either way would be dangerous.

'Why would San Wu want some white woman? Who is she anyway?'

'You know perfectly well who she is — news of her has spread to the mountains, I know this. Do not play dumb.' Abau's patience was beginning to wane. The substance was morphing his mood into something ugly and unpredictable.

'Say I do know — why would San Wu pay for her when I can take her for nothing?'

'You would not last a second. Get the money. You go and tell your precious leader that we have her. He will pay. Or I cannot be responsible for what happens to her.' Abau had pulled his knife and was pointing it with shaking hands in the vicinity of Eve's neck. She murmured with pain as it scratched her skin.

'Hey, easy there now, big man. No need for that. I do not make the decisions for San Wu — nobody does.' The blood was starting to pulsate at his temple. It was not going to be as easy as he first thought.

'You tell that sniveling little idiot that I will kill her if he does not want her. She is no use to me.' Abau pushed the small figure into an alcove in the dark and sprang at Josefo with the knife pointed directly at his stomach. The small figure wriggled into a corner, hugging the pavement.

Even though the kidnapper was larger, Josefo had skilful hands and speed with a knife. He drew the small blade from his belt, maneuvered his legs between those of the bigger man, twisted, and from behind forced him to the ground — the knife now at his throat. Taken aback by the speed and strength of his assailant, Abau lashed out with the machete, barely scraping the skin of Josefo's arm.

Josefo's first kill had not been easy. In most cases it was warranted, relieving the world of a vile character that didn't deserve to breathe. But he didn't want to kill this one. Over time he'd developed a kind of friendship with this younger brother of the two he had met many times. He, like Josefo, had his reason for wanting money, an opposing reason to his own, but to him the reason was valid. Who was Josefo to judge which side was right? We all have a cause, he thought. But tonight Abau showed different colors.

'Sorry, friend. I just do not have that much cash on me tonight and besides, I have never had to pay for a woman.' He almost laughed aloud at the thought. In his humor, he lost focus, and the man pushed the knife further toward him. Josefo's reactions were swifter than his brain. His small jungle knife embedded itself into the large pulsating area of Abau's neck that was the jugular. Red, sticky fluid sprouted. The man gurgled and his head fell back. A faint murmur came from behind the shadows of the pillar.

Josefo was transfixed and stood motionless, looking at the dead man's head swimming in blood. He reached inside Abau's coat and pulled out the bag he had passed over earlier. If he were clever, he may be able to negotiate a deal sometime before they got back to camp. San Wu would not be pleased. He might get away with not mentioning it if not for the woman. But she had to live. He'd have to wait it out and see how his persuasive skills worked. He'd talked himself out of situations before, he could do it again. But it was another mistake he couldn't afford. At this rate, he would never get his promotion — not unless someone died.

The murmuring in the darkness had grown louder. They had to move quickly.

He untied the ropes from the woman's hands but decided to leave the tape on her mouth.

'Shh — just listen — that was an accident. I did not mean to kill him but things happen. We have to move. Be quiet and keep calm. I am not going to harm you. I take you to San Wu. He a good guy, like me.'

He thought a smile might be helpful but decided against it. Slowly and gently he took away the tape from her mouth — the skin was red and raw around it — not a pretty sight. Cameras can lie, he thought.

'Abau,' said the woman as she looked over at the man's body in the darkness.

'That was his name. Son of Ko Tan, yes.'

Then she added, 'Please don't kill me!'

'Of course not — you are valuable. I am Josefo. You are Eve.'

She collapsed in front of him. There would be problems with this one.

11

Dottmar felt a burning in her chest; a constriction that did not go away. She had noticed it the first day Eve was gone, disappeared from their lives as quickly as she had appeared. She had awoken one morning, gone to Eve's room as usual to call her for breakfast and remembered she had said her goodbyes the night before. She looked at the room, as empty as it had been for many years, yet after only a couple of weeks, her presence remained. As she left the room she now liked to call Eve's, her throat grew tight and her eyes welled with tears.

She walked out to the terrace where Ko Tan was waiting, with Mya nearby.

'Ko Tan — she is really gone. She was here for such a short time.' She stared at Ko Tan, her eyes not focusing.

'We should have insisted on taking her to the airport — it was so late.' Ko Tan said as Mya walked around the table. She whispered into Ko Tan's ear. He looked at Dottmar.

'What is it, Ko Tan?'

'Mya has something she wants to tell us. Mya?'

'I saw her leave, Ma'am. She was running — with Abau. They were in a hurry!'

'Why did you not tell us before?'

'I did not think it was my place, Ma'am. Really, do not be angry!'

How could Dottmar get angry with this wretched girl? There was no use in questioning her, if she didn't want to speak she certainly couldn't make her. Ko Tan may be able to get something out of her.

'What are you suggesting, Mya? Abau and Eve? No, surely not. She didn't even seem to like him. Ko Tan, there is more to this, I can feel it.' Dottmar clenched and unclenched her fingers, her nails digging into the soft flesh of her palms. Ko Tan got up and walked towards the door.

'She is probably on her way back to Australia now and Abau just helped her get to the airport. He is helpful in that way.'

The manservant appeared with a tray of croissants and coffee.

'Oh I am not hungry — take the tray away, please.' Dottmar felt there was something missing from the story. She could not believe Eve had wanted to be with Abau. There was something wrong. She had never expected the young woman to leave like this, she appeared responsible, reliable, she would have told them, surely. She left Ko Tan and Mya in the courtyard and went back to her room where she lay on her bed and looked out of her picture window to the valley below.

She didn't enjoy feeling this way, never wanted it nor encouraged it. She had banished this feeling from her life and didn't want it back. But back it was, the yearning pain that had driven itself into her heart all those years ago and had been slowly building ever since. With Eve's entrance into her life, she was reminded of the daughter she had left behind. She had successfully ignored it, had convinced herself that her daughter no longer existed. She had given birth, of course, that she could never forget. But she had forgotten her own child, its growing personality, its strength of will and its soul. It was no longer an it, she had taken possession of Dottmar a lot longer ago than she cared to admit, and there was no ridding herself of this feeling that would be with her for life. It had been with her all these years, she had just managed to stifle the feelings of love growing within her. These feelings of love she didn't want to own if she couldn't see her daughter. If she couldn't see her, she didn't exist. Simple. But she did exist, was real, had a soul, a body and a beautiful face that had been nurtured in a country far from here. Then Eve came into her life.

Dottmar thought about Eve, this woman from across the world who had intruded on her schedule. Dottmar's life was planned and the plan no longer included emotion for someone else. She had noticed her feelings for Eve had grown and she was confused by the increasing attachment she felt for the younger woman. Instead of frustration and anger she had felt a stirring of emotion. An attachment certainly — but love? She sensed sadness in Eve's eyes. She wanted to take Eve, hold her, protect her. Protect her from herself and her anxieties Dottmar had noticed in the young woman. It was the Robinson curse. Never to have happiness, only regret. She had seen the same in Alex, something buried deep beneath the surface but she knew would evolve into reality when he was least expecting it. But that could change.

She had seen the timidity in the young woman and a sense of other worldness, as if she was here and yet not here. Dottmar recognized her fear and wondered how she had hidden her insecurities all these years. She was by all accounts a successful scientist. She wondered how an anxious young woman lived such a parallel life. She remembered her own nervousness at the truth being revealed — there was so much Dottmar needed to know, wanted to ask her. She wanted to tell her about her past, be honest. She no longer wanted to pretend. Dottmar had only known Eve a short time but she could not lose her. She had to be part of her life.

The past had risen up to strike at this time of her life when she had settled comfortably in a pattern, a suitable arrangement that could go on calmly in balance and harmony. But even before Eve had come into her home, her heart had begun to feel different about her surroundings, her life, her domain. Its cause was a young maidservant brought into the house not so many years ago to tear her apart and steal her husband

Dottmar lay on the bed, her eyes open and her heart pounding. She was worried, she could not deny it even though she kept telling herself that Eve was an adult, could look after herself and was probably on a plane destined for home. Her senses did not let her rest. She rose from the bed and shuffled to the telephone table. The phone directory for the city of Rangoon was enormous. She went directly to airlines, Australian, Qantas. She didn't know but had to assume that was the carrier Eve used. She found the Qantas number, dialed and waited. Had there been any flights to Australia in the last 12 hours? She knew the airlines wouldn't divulge names but finally came off the phone knowing there had been scheduled flights to several Australian cities the night before. Had Eve caught the plane or was she still in the country? She may have checked into a hotel. Yet Dottmar felt that she had not boarded a plane. Eve was still here — wherever 'here' was.

And the source of this profound information that she had abandoned them? Mya, the maid, the woman who had stolen her husband, almost a child. This young maid could not be trusted. Dottmar had felt this long ago but could not gather any evidence to prove it. The girl did not leave proof of her habits. It was a feeling she had about the girl. She was dishonest and deceitful. Anyone would be if they actively pursued the husband of another woman and shared his bed in her own house! Could she blame her? Mya was an opportunist who saw a vacant space in the bed next to, she presumed, the owner of the homestead and the keeper of the purse strings. How wrong she was! She couldn't bring herself to blame Ko Tan for his infidelity. She had shunned him early in their marriage. He was always a loving man, kind, a perfect husband until he realized that his wife would continue to ignore him no matter what he did. She was immune to whatever charms he possessed.

Eve knew no one else in Rangoon — only the people she'd met in the house. Dottmar needed to speak to Abau. If the maidservant was right and could be believed, Abau was the last to be seen with Eve that night.

Abau's room was at the other end of the corridor next to the Rose Room. She looked at her watch. Not yet dinner time. Abau was probably in his room preparing the evening's transmissions scheduled for after dinner. There may even be some news on the wire about the foreigner. Dottmar got up quickly and walked out into the long hallway that ended in a teardrop shape at the entrance hall. Abau's room was not as far down. She could see the thin slit of light from under his door so knew him to be in his room as she had suspected. She approached and knocked lightly. There was no sound, no movement from within. She knocked again a little louder this time while twisting the doorknob and easing the door open. She hesitated before she did this, remembering the time when her son had been in his room entertaining a young woman who was perched on top of him like an equestrienne. She had never again dared to open the door without invitation — his wrath was frightening even to his own mother.

As she had heard no movement, she felt it was safe and opened the door to reveal an empty room, at least empty of life, of Abau. What she did find was alarming and surprising enough to warrant her screaming for Ko Tan to come immediately.

'Ko Tan — look!'

Abau's room had been ransacked, drawers pulled out, mattress overturned and clothes strewn all over the floor.

'Oh my god — what has he got himself into now!'

*

Mya concealed herself behind a large column which held the structure of the house in place directly in front of the library opposite Abau's room. She knew the layout of his room well even though she was not in view of it. She could picture the small old-fashioned sash window and the child's desk with matching wardrobe that no one, least of all Abau, had ever bothered to replace as he was growing older. She knew that a tall lamp with a rose-colored shade stood in the corner of the room which was more often used as a tallboy for disheveled jackets than as a vehicle to provide light. The multi-colored Egyptian rug had fascinated her as she watched it from above and saw the myriad colors merging into a jungle kaleidoscope. Even the bed itself, an old-style child's three-quarter bed not quite large enough to hold two people in Mya's mind but most often used for that purpose, she knew would be unmade, sheets unwashed and pillows akimbo. An old digital clock radio would be by the bed on a small light-colored wooden bedside table, its width barely providing room for the clock and of all things, a bible. That part of Abau's tastes surprised her, far more than his other tastes with which she had become familiar.

Mya had not had any intelligence about Abau or Eve. She could tell by the way they had moved through the courtyard that Eve was not a willing participant in any scheme Abau had planned. His plans were often failures and if this one too had failed, she would not be surprised. Or concerned for either party. The white woman would only cause trouble for her grand plan. She had nearly succeeded in overcoming Dottmar's power and would soon be the woman of the house. It was only a matter of time. As long as the white woman stayed missing, she could continue her plan. It wouldn't take long for information to come directly to her. She had only to wait. In the meantime, she had to sow the seed that the Australian had gone willingly with Abau. If anything had happened to him, she could be blamed for this too. Mya decided the white woman should disappear permanently.

12

The hard ground crunched under their feet. It had been unseasonally dry. Usually it was constant rain pounding on the dirt, turning it into mud and slush. The jungle drank in the warm wetness of the seasons and prospered under the canopy of protection. The track was obscured by branches which strong hands had to push to clear for the others to follow. Most feet were badly covered, wet from rain and slush. The shoes, if they had any, were the wrong size and torn, worn out at the sole with empty lace holes. Within these shoes the feet were blistered and bleeding, some with no socks to layer the rough leather between. The small ones felt it the most. Short steps and slow, they couldn't keep up with the large feet which had to wait, holding up the line. Sometimes the small feet just stopped and fell amidst the undergrowth and mud. Usually they were noticed and picked up off the ground to be carried for some of the way until the carrier too gave way under the load. Most of the time, they would fall and not be seen in the undergrowth, would be trampled by the oncoming line of feet and buried beneath the jungle floor.

The march had been underway for months.

Different feet had walked this path but always the same path. From their beloved mountains, they were marching to the lowlands to settle in another village.

Whole families started the journey — most didn't finish.

Papa Chau Lap looked up from the muddy track and turned to see the line of his community behind him. He could not see the end of the line. The trees and jungle growth were thick, the line of people extended beyond his sight. He'd had his whole family at the start of the journey two months before. Since then, he had lost his youngest daughter and oldest son to dysentery. His remaining son still coughed up blood on the track and was very weak but he was alive. Mama Chau Lap had given up long ago and had stayed behind in a small community along the track.

'Come and get me when you are settled,' she had said. But Papa Chau Lap knew he would not be able to go back. She was lost to him. He kept walking.

He hoped that after the next month, the remaining members of his community could rebuild their lives in the new village and put the long march behind them. The new crop would be waiting.

13

Eve awoke to the sound of crashing. She could barely move and seemed to be restrained in a small compartment. She felt the incessant drum of an engine directly below her and her mouth and lungs gasped for air. At first, she thought she was at home among her beloved tree crop, hearing the roar of the crop duster above her spreading the fertilizer over the great brown landscape of inland Australia.

Her head swam slightly and her body ached from the inside out. She became aware of shouting and realized that she was not in Australia and not safe. The events of the evening came back. Abau forcing her into the dark laneways of the village. The struggle in the dark — the attacker killing Abau. Talk of money and San Wu. The dark man, the killer, had taken her. How would she be found? Where were they going?

Again she tried to move her leaden legs, her hips were sore and her mouth was parched. She reached out in front of her and found herself to be free although she saw large red welts around her wrists and felt the raw pain of freshly grazed skin. At least I'm not tied up like a Christmas ham, she thought.

She felt a rising heat within herself and realized it was fear. Who was this man who killed Abau right in front of her eyes? The rocking motion of her surroundings together with the drumming of the engine told her she was probably on a light plane. A larger one would not be so unstable. As there was no escape at the moment, there was no alternative but to talk to her captor and find out what use she was to him. This all seemed like a fantasy she was dreaming. But everything was real. She moved her shaking arms and sore wrists to her side and slowly eased herself out of what seemed to be a curved bunk — perhaps one of those rescue beds she'd seen on American adventure movies.

She forced her legs to the floor and steadied herself with the help of the bunk. It was no easy process with the movement of the plane going against her wishes. She checked her body for other injuries. A few scratches, definitely aches and pains but no major wounds or dried blood. Her clothes were dirty and disheveled but still there — relief. She moved towards a closed door in front of her. The room she found herself in felt more like a cabin on a ship — if she had been any taller she would have been unable to stand up in the space. At least there were some advantages to being short.

Before she reached the door, Eve stopped. What was she going to do if faced with that dark man again? How did she expect to get out of this? Should she plan a strategy? Eve was used to passing tests with very little preparation — her photographic memory had served her well over the years and given her a confidence she had never expected. But here was a situation that could not be planned. She felt the familiar irregular patter of her heart, and a heat in her face that would not go away.

She pushed the door and, on its resistance, turned the handle. Slowly the door opened onto a sight that she would not soon forget. What first met her lowered gaze was pure white shag pile carpet. She hadn't seen this since she was a child. The walls were a rich dark red, almost magenta as its base. The cabin was large and unlike the interior of any plane she had ever seen.

Dotted around the open area were white leather lounges straddled on either side by champagne buckets. The lighting was soft, produced by two tall gold-shaded and tasseled lamps fastened to the floor. In the middle of the room was a glass cabinet full of every type of alcohol.

In the midst of this ambience of white and red, a man was seated on one of the leather lounges. He was propped forward, leaning into the glass-topped table and shoveling powder into his nose. Eve had been to parties where there was the inevitable dope circle (in which she was never included) but she had never witnessed anyone snorting what had to be cocaine. She'd only seen it on television. While the man snorted happily, a younger man sat awkwardly on the other sofa. He was dark, young and looked worried. Not worried exactly, she thought, just uncomfortable.

As she stood at the door, the two men became aware of her and the worried expression of the younger man washed away to be replaced by a dashing smile. He'd had good dental care, she noticed. Strangely, she felt her mouth begin to shape into a mirrored response but stopped herself before it was born. She could never be friendly to these people; they had kidnapped her.

The younger man lifted himself from the lounge and came towards her. She recognized him as the man who had killed Abau and the familiar heat in her chest began to rise. Her hands began to shake again.

'You killed Abau', she said.

As her words filled the space, the older man looked up from his powder, wiped his nose, leant back in his sofa and laughed.

'Do not be afraid — come and sit — have some water.' The young man led her to the leather lounge, sat her down and poured some water into a glass from the carafe on the table.

'Please believe that it was an accident. I did not mean to kill Abau. He was a friend!' He looked at the older man and smiled. 'By the way, he is not the pilot!' The man laughed again taking another line of powder.

She remembered his face in the dark and now she recalled his name, Josefo. Had he kidnapped her or saved her — she wasn't sure.

'What happened to him — his body? It's so terrible leaving it there!' Eve thought of the many dogs that roamed the plaza and felt sick.

'Do not worry — we took care of it.' She didn't want to get into details and just hoped his body was secure.

'What do you want with me? I'm just a tourist!'

'Do not be so modest. You are much more than that, some people believe anyway. I am just the messenger to get you an audience with our great leader of the freedom movement. San Wu wants to meet you.'

'I don't know any San Wu! I'm only here trying to find out about my father. Please tell me what's happening — where are we going and why?'

'It will not take long. Only a couple more hours and we will be at our border landing, then a short journey in our limo service and we are there. I will get food.'

Josefo mumbled something unintelligible to the other man who extricated himself from his seat and slipped past her into the room from which she'd just emerged.

'My friend will get you food.' She suddenly felt hungry.

'I hear you from Australia. What is it like there? I mean to go.'

Eve thought it strange making small talk under these circumstances. She paused for a moment wanting to hold back, be silent, difficult.

'You've just kidnapped me and you expect me to do small talk?'

Josefo had the wide eyes of an inquisitive boy. Eve looked at him closely now that she could see him unobscured by darkness as the fear subsided into hunger.

He wasn't tall, he didn't tower over Eve. She could tell he had a lithe body under his black skivvy and green camouflage pants. Very Che Guevara, she thought. He moved quickly and with ease. His face was charcoal, framed by jet black and occasional curls. She moved her eyes down his body, noticing his taut, well-developed upper arms and torso. Her eyes stopped at his hands. The skin was white patchwork on dark with many scars showing white against his skin. She looked away.

He looked at his hands.

'I am fighter, not killer. Not often anyway. I am good with knives but stay away from other people's.'

'So what happened with Abau — you shouldn't have killed him. He wasn't going to hurt me. I knew him!'

'We should call you "naïve Eve". Wake up! He was to trade you for cash until I talked him out of it.'

'Yes, by sticking a knife in his neck. His parents will be destroyed!'

She wondered what the reaction would be back at the house. How could she explain that she didn't make it to the airport, that she was an innocent victim? Ko Tan and Dottmar would be devastated by their loss.

Yet, if what Josefo said was true and San Wu wanted to meet her, she may be able to discover something more about the origin of the freedom movement, maybe even learn something about her father and what he was hiding from her.

She remembered that Ko Tan had mentioned San Wu in passing one night. 'He believes he has freed his people — in fact, he has done the opposite.' He used the words 'eccentric', 'passionate', 'angry', 'brutal', 'caring'. What was closest to the truth, she wondered.

'What's he like, this San Wu?' Eve posed the question to her fellow traveler.

'I can tell you about him later. Now you need food — and rest. We have some hard work ahead.'

*

Josefo looked at this benign foreign woman. Though she was probably a few years older than he, he felt light years ahead of her. One look at her hands told him she hadn't done much physical work, no scarring to speak of and he could tell she was the nervous type. It had been a long time since he had met someone who had not been brought up in the grip of civil war and bloodshed. It was too long ago for him to remember days free of fear and a life in one place. Nowadays, no one lived anywhere for long, locations were kept secret and ever-changing. It was too risky to trust or befriend those one knew, less secure still to trust a stranger.

The older man came through the small door holding a bowl of food — some rice and pieces of meat. She ate quickly.

'Once we get to the landing strip, we wash and change clothes for the drive to the border. You rest now. I wake you before we land. I hope you like walking!'

14

Standing outside Abau's room, Mya darted a look in Ko Tan's direction and caught his eye unexpectedly.

'What is it, Mya? Do you know something about what has happened to Abau's room?'

Her body slouched and she took on the cowering countenance she used in situations where she needed to appear vulnerable, alone and young.

'I do not know anything, Ko Tan — I just thought you knew ...' She stopped short at what they might know as Dottmar twisted around to face her.

'Knew what — tell us, girl. This is no time to play coy.'

'Come on, Mya, it is alright, please tell us,' cajoled Ko Tan.

'I have seen them together, as friends, as ... more than friends. I thought you knew that ... they seem to be missing together, yes? And I saw them together two nights ago heading toward the village.' She stopped to let the news sink in, hoping they would not think it preposterous that a woman like the serious Australian would go with a loose cannon like Abau. She had to test it.

They nibbled the bait, it tasted good until it got to

the hook. There they stuck. Perfect.

'Eve and Abau — no! Ko Tan! What can we do?' Dottmar became more upset as Ko Tan put his arm around her to comfort her.

'What is the matter?' Mya's interest was growing with something potentially new to add to her information.

'Nothing, Mya. Dottmar, we must call the police.' Mya had to think fast.

'But Ko Tan, Sir, she will be an alien with no papers. This may not be good. If they find her, before you can vouch for her, she will be in big trouble.' Mya watched for the reaction.

Ko Tan pondered on this, both surprised and concerned that Mya had spotted something so obvious, yet he hadn't seen it.

'She is right, Dottmar. We must get some information first about what has happened, then we will know what to do.'

15

The landing strip ran parallel with the compound near the base of the mountains. They disembarked and made their way to the small building. Eve entered a room with an adjoining bathroom and opened the wardrobe. She was surprised to find an array of clothing to fit most sizes. She had been instructed to choose both light and heavy clothing and some sturdy boots. Before she had left Australia, she had been shopping for hiking boots but couldn't find any comfortable enough or small enough for her feet. She had fossicked through the wardrobe and found a small pair of well-worn brown ankle boots with a solid toe and ankle support. They fitted well on the first try. So much for designer outdoor clothing shops, she thought.

She salvaged a couple of T-shirts and long-sleeved ex-army shirts from the pile. Outside, Josefo was waiting by the so-called limo which turned out to be a 20-year-old jeep. At one time no doubt it had been fitted with roof and doors but now was bereft of both. The bonnet and existing side panels were not only severely dented but exhibited the pockmarked hide of an animal hit by rounds of lead pellets. Eve felt her heart quicken. What sort of people were these who had to dodge bullets? Were they going into a war zone? Eve started to panic — this was raw fear, real fear she could almost touch. She was used to Saturday morning beach walks, lunch with her father occasionally, dinner at home with Roger.

The mountain's jungle tracks were patrolled by the infamous Wa people, Josefo had explained. They were simple people who had been turned into guerillas and trained by the government to protect the borders. Every son from every village family was conscripted into this vigilante group. Most families never saw their sons again — nor would they have wanted to witness what they had become. Lost forever were the innocent young men providing water and crops for their families. Now they were dangerous killing machines who did not hesitate to destroy property, families, children. These young men were part of a different family which consisted only of the cold, hard, metal grasped in their hands, men held together by fear.

'This is where we leave you, my friend. See you on my next trip.' Josefo patted the older man on the back. In response, he gave a trumpeting inhalation of air followed by unsightly matter coming from the man's long-suffering nose. The sputum landed on the ground near Eve's foot.

'The cocaine catches me,' guffawed his compatriot.

'You should stick to tobacco — it is better for your health, and cheaper!'

Eve, watching silently by the jeep, felt her stomach roll over at this sight she had heard of but never actually witnessed. So the habit was true. She would know to stay well clear when she heard this sound again.

The man turned around and padded back to his lodgings next to the plane. She didn't know what long-term effect cocaine had on a person's abilities and she didn't want to find out.

'A great pilot, yes?' Josefo laughed loudly at his private joke, something she had started to notice he did often. She was panicked again at how the pilot could have been flying the plane, doing lines of cocaine and fixing her meal at the same time until she looked back at the plane to see a third man organizing the refueling and jumping into the cockpit waving at the group. Josefo winked.

'I will drive — do not want us to get lost.' Josefo looked amused as he put the key in the ignition.

'Are you sure you've never been to Australia?' Eve enjoyed her own little joke but he stared blankly back at her. Most arguments she'd had with boyfriends had involved a steering wheel and a map.

'Get comfortable — we will be driving for a few hours and the road is no beauty — hold on.'

Once in the jeep with an incalculable amount of gear and equipment loaded in the back, Eve discovered her hands were no longer shaking.

16

E ve's childhood was happy and yet she had constant anxiety which manifested itself in headaches and flashes of panic which she could not pin down to any one event. The only reason she was successful in her career — however that was measured — was the fact that she didn't make a decision. She kept on studying as it seemed the only option. Studying and the academic life came easily to a person who did not connect with her peers, who was an outsider. She did a master's, 'and why not a PhD while I'm at it?' she thought. It certainly delayed that inevitable question of 'what will you do when you grow up?' She was happy with the concept of never finishing. The irony was she had no distractions so she didn't finish. It was her ongoing promise to herself, turning into her lifetime goal. When people asked her how it was going, she turned away. The people who knew, the people in academia, pitied her lack of drive to get it finished. Others outside that world respected and idolized her, though she didn't meet many of those. Horticulture had been her passion from an early age, although she didn't call it that. Her love of nasturtiums, jonquils and frangipani around their rambling home had brought her a joy that nothing could match. The trees around her home had been a comfort to her; mulberry, date palm, the fine eucalypt, the sprawling tea tree hedge, and the fruits from the loquat, lemon, plum, and apple trees, with the curvaceous grapevine. Crawling through them, on them and above them all brought her pleasure she could not describe.

Her father, Alex, had been an omniscient being, ever watchful yet keeping an emotional distance that she found comforting. He had told her that her mother had died in an accident. The fact that there were no photographs or mementos of any kind scarcely drew her curiosity. She simply believed what he'd told her — that he had lost many possessions in a house fire when she was a year old. There were no photographs of him in his early years. All the photographs were of Eve — and plenty of them. At every stage of her life, there was a collectable library of captured memories adorning the house like decorative beacons. Alex had added to the photos year by year — so much that she began to tire of seeing herself.

Alex couldn't show affection — she found that out long ago. The mere touch of her finger against his larger hand had made him shy away. He was fearful, she thought, of getting too close to the daughter he loved like a mother dog with her new born pup. He needn't have worried. She knew he loved her. His quiet way had been her life. Both of them were involved in their own introspective worlds. He in his daily 9 to 5 of a clerkship in a shipping company, and she buried deep within her studies.

His job had colored him grey although he seemed to be content in his ordinariness. Sometimes she longed for him to take more than a passing interest in her passion, to participate in her life other than merely sharing a meal, risk his heart and mind in the pursuit of something unknown. Why did she wish it for him if she didn't believe she had it for herself?

Early in her life, she had noticed her dizzy spells and anxiety attacks but they had gained in intensity and frequency during her doctorate. Her father remained unaware of her symptoms but she felt that she needed some medical advice. The campus doctor wasn't much older than she and had studied at the same campus — medicine, of course, not horticulture.

'But I love gardening,' Roger had told her. Even though he stereotyped her scientific career, she somehow felt a connection. She'd mentioned the anxiety and the frequency of attacks. He'd prescribed Zoloft. She'd never heard of it. But it turned into her savior. And Roger. What she tried to deny was the reason they married so soon after meeting. It had been six weeks. She told herself she was in love, he was the perfect man — handsome, tall, intelligent, liked her — a lot. He said. To others, his lips disappeared into a cavernous mouth, large feathery eyebrows hung over small black eyes which constantly darted to and fro like a small furry animal, his body stooped, tall and angular. At first she loved his hands, big, rigid, flexible, strong. He caressed her knowingly with those hands. There had been others but this one was witty, sensitive and caring. Her father liked him. She struggled to remember their first meeting. It didn't go well but not many meetings did with her father. She had managed to hear him say, 'Marry if you want to — it's a good thing to do,' before he had turned back to the crossword which he was well on the way to finishing. He wouldn't let it beat him.

When the crash came for Eve two years before, it came hard. Everything she knew turned upside down. She left her studies, her science, her passion. Became a gardener to old women, just what Roger had assumed she was at the beginning. She avoided all contact with people and was happiest among her plants. It wouldn't last, she would resume her passion. Just not yet.

17

By the time they'd been driving for a couple of hours, Eve was sweating. Not from panic, but from the heat.

'How do you do it?' she asked Josefo.

'Do what?'

'Get used to the heat. I know I'm from Australia but we have a dryness there that I can tolerate — not this incessant sweating that drains your very soul. Do you ever get used to it?'

He could see she looked uncomfortable which was not surprising in her circumstances, he thought.

'I was born in the city but grew up in the mountains. Not far from where we are headed. San Wu knew my father.' He had been glancing at her in between concentrating on the track then looked away. 'When you have been here a long time, it very natural. The heat is part of you and, the sweat wash away the dirt. We do not wash much.' He smiled wryly to himself waiting to see what she would say.

'I can tell.' He threw her a sideways glance.

'It was tough for my family. We harvested poppies and then the government made us leave our beloved land. It going for years. You work your life to feed your family and the crops are taken. You do not get back what they are worth, believe me. When the harvest is bad and we cannot pay, they take something else. They take the children.'

Eve looked at him. His eyes showed no flutter of feeling at this revelation.

'I've heard that but I didn't believe it. Why can't they just wait until the harvest is ready and then take their pick?' She knew the answer already.

'They have their rules.'

'How did San Wu know your father? Did you grow up near each other?' Eve felt she was encroaching on unsteady ground but decided to pursue it. Her heart was beating fast but she felt no dizziness.

He didn't answer for a long time. Then he turned to her.

'San Wu was the leader of the guerillas who ripped my sister from the womb of her family. I have not seen her for ten years.'

'That's shocking! How could you work for a man who has done that to your family? Did you ever try to find her?'

'I had no choice. This is not the west, Eve. Remember.'

It was the first time he'd called her by name. It felt as warm as ice blocks in lemonade.

'We are in for some rough terrain so stay in your seat!' She took that as a sign that talking was over.

Eve had overheard that they had flown about 800 kilometers between the two major cities from south to north. The landing strip had provided the base in the center of the entire region and they were now moving across land toward the border and San Wu's hub, probably another 400 kilometers.

Eve had to hang on to the railing above her head for most of the journey as no seat belts were provided and there was no way of being harnessed. It was hang on or be thrown. The track was rugged. Passing through the dirt was like maneuvering a double decker bus through a cobbled lane in Rome. But most of the time Josefo forged through. He was solemn and did not speak again for several hours. In the meantime, she swallowed the landscape that was so different from her own. The vast, brown-tinged scrub and dusty red sand of the Australian bush was replaced here with lush tropical forest overhead and dark brown, rich sludgy soil beneath (which she had to wipe constantly from her face). If she'd seen her image, she would have thought she had just been in a chocolate meringue throwing contest. Though it seemed they were driving at breakneck speed, when she looked at the speedo it showed 30 km. At this rate, she thought, they would be here for days.

They passed through a few small villages though they never stopped, just sped by leaving wet pods of mud in their wake.

'We are stopping for the night,' Josefo announced as the jeep slowed and stopped in a small clearing off the main track. 'There is a freshwater stream here and I can pitch two tents. We will have to start early in the morning. Start unpacking the jeep.'

She didn't like the way he gave orders. It reminded her too much of Roger who was pushing his way into her thoughts. She did as she was told and laid the gear on top of a tarpaulin she'd found to protect it from the dirty ground.

As Josefo fussed over the tent hitching she thought about all those girl guide sessions she had missed at school. They'd have come in handy now, she mused. It was still light and Josefo had pointed out the freshwater stream to her indicating that it was a good time for her to wash. She grabbed some soap and washcloths and another shirt, and found herself at the water's edge. She looked around carefully before removing most of her clothing and immersing herself in the clear cool water peppered with smoothed rocks and a shimmering surface. She looked about her, at once alert and soothed.

The tropical diseases unit back home had told her to be careful when swimming in mountainous streams in tropical climates. The organisms swimming in the water had other malevolent intentions — to get into your insides and eat their way out. She blotted the dangers from her mind and considered her potentially life-threatening predicament. She didn't feel in danger from Josefo and she had learnt from the past to go with her instincts. The swim had erased the clamminess and dried sweat on her body. After dressing, she returned to the camp to find a blazing fire with something already cooking on the stove.

'You really know how to entertain in the jungle — you've been doing this a long time!' She smiled despite herself and he returned the compliment with a wide, white grin in a dark brown face.

'Sit now and we eat — we have pig's ear and soya beans.' Josefo dived into the pot with a fork and grabbed some meat which he placed on a plate and gave to Eve.

'Tell me more about your life in the jungle and how you came to be here.' Eve was curious about this man and she had no choice but to make conversation.

'I was born outside Mandalay with a sister, brothers and parents. My parents are dead, my brothers went into the army and I am looking for my sister.' He told her about his life, the hardships of his people and how he had to break out on his own to survive.

Then he was silent, looking into the flames of the fire. It was a while before he spoke again.

'It had been an ordinary day in the village. We had collected the water, fed the animals, and rounded up the chickens as we always did. Marinda was with me — she was 14 years old. She did not like being in the chicken coop — she said she hurt the chicken's sleeping. She had a favorite called Galay. She would visit Galay every day, stroke his broad feathers and whisper to him. I wanted to know what she said to him, but she would not tell. That day in the chicken coop, the chickens were more restless — their feathers flew as we chased them into their pens, as they ran in circles to what would soon be the end. Marinda was upset by the chicken's noises and that her Galay had to be herded into the yard. She did not hear the sound of feet on damp ground.

It is her laughter I still hear — not her screams. They tore her from the coop, bundled her into a sack and threw her on the back of a truck packed with other squirming bundles of black canvas.

'The soldiers have come again — it is inevitable,' my mother had said. 'The opium is not enough for them — they must take the children.' She tried to calm me. 'Do not worry, Josefo. She will be fed and clothed. It is more than we can do for her. It is the opium we must protect.'

That night I knew I could no longer stay in the house of my mother, living from the sale of children. I no longer felt like a child, I had to look after myself.'

Eve had tears in her eyes and was compelled to reach out to him, touch his hand, his face. She felt his tears on her fingertips.

Josefo recoiled from her touch. He wasn't used to females getting close, certainly not in an emotional way. He had not had any trouble with the physical side of relationships. In fact he craved it, especially in the jungle camps when he was on patrol for weeks at a time.

He found opportunities.

But any show of emotion was another thing. Not once could he remember being hugged by his parents. They were too busy keeping the farm going and tending to their crops. Just keeping the crops alive was back-breaking work and often they were too tired even to communicate with each other at the end of the day. In his early life the only one who had ever told Josefo she loved him was Marinda, his beloved sister. So often he thought about that day in the barn and with such sorrow that he found it hard to awake to the day and to continue breathing. Over the years, part of him had managed to heal on the inside, yet there was still something missing. His later life did not have room for love or real closeness with another human being. Being on the run and working for San Wu meant he could trust no one.

His three older brothers had been conscripted early — even before his memory of them. They had been taken to fight for the cause. He had never seen them again.

Strangely, even in the short few hours they had traveled together, he had begun to like this strange, foreign woman. She wasn't unattractive though she did not have the exotic charm of a local woman. She lacked mystery, everything was in the open.

His people were like another species. Untrusting, secretive, hiding their feelings even from those they loved — this was normal to him and to everyone he knew. He remembered one dry season when the crops had been slow to harvest. He did not understand the pressure on his father at the time, the pressure to yield a certain amount or face the consequences. He did not know what those consequences were. All he knew was that he had finished school for the term and had brought his report to show his father, pulling out the yellow card that displayed the marks he knew were the highest in his class. His father had looked down at him and to the paper in his hand. He ha snatched the paper, torn it into small pieces and tossed it into the wind.

'This is what I think of your schooling. No son of mine wastes his time at school when there is work to be done on the farm. That is the last you will see of school. You know enough.' His father turned toward the rows of crops, looked at the boy and signaled him to follow. Josefo did not return to school.

Looking back he figured he had not missed much. His schooling was the school of life and the jungle. He had learned about farming the poppies and their harvest. Only later would he come to know their value on the open market. Then, as a young man in San Wu's care, he had learned the valuable skills of weapons handling, military tactics, and jungle craft — skills far more useful to him than reading and writing. He thanked his father every day for that choice.

His mother had only had time to speak to him as she was placing the night's food on the table for his sister and him. His father did not share mealtimes as he was still cleaning and putting away the equipment for the night. He took his meal later and alone. After school had finished for Josefo, his days were filled with the crop and the farm. He did not think there would be anything else and was satisfied with that. And then they took her.

'I do not like to be touched on my face,' he said to Eve. She pulled her hand away.

'I feel sad for you ... and for your sister. What did you say her name was?'

'Marinda.' As he said her name, he buried his hand deep within his shirt and the hair of his chest, pulling out something that looked like a coin.

'This was our only childhood gift from our parents. They gave us two halves of an ancient emblem engraved on silver — half for Marinda and half for me. Each attached to a chain. We wore it always as two halves of one soul.' He held out the silver talisman to Eve and she turned it slowly in her hand, feeling the warmth of his body in its face.

'I think I have seen this before somewhere but I can't think where ...'

'That is not possible. It is very rare. My parents told me they had traded with a gypsy who had access to the very finest and unique items in Burma. Where could you have seen it?'

Eve tried to picture where she may have seen such a piece of jewelry. Around a woman's neck? She created the image in her mind and slowly, the face of Mya appeared above the silver emblem.

'It was Ko Tan's maid!' she exclaimed. 'Her name is Mya and she works in the old house for Ko Tan and his family. She must be your sister!' Eve, excited by the revelation, was shocked by Josefo's change of expression.

'Mya? A maid? No member of my family serves another. You must be mistaken.'

'No, I don't think so. When I first went to the house, I met Mya, who showed me to my room. As she was handing me my clothes, I noticed her unusual necklace. She didn't want to talk about it and tucked it under her blouse so I wouldn't see it again. She was very embarrassed and left the room flustered. I thought it odd at the time but let it go from my memory. It has to be related. Why would she be so nervous about it?'

'Did you see it closely?

'I saw it was definitely a half of another — it was

broken as yours is — yes, it was the matching half.'

Josefo thought about the possibility that this was true. He felt a strangeness in himself that he couldn't explain and then his body began to shake. He raised himself from the fire and walked to the edge of the stream. There he allowed himself to cry, tears of longing for family and forgiveness.

If I lose myself I have nothing. I want it all yet I want nothing. The fear of losing myself and my worth came from losing my family and my beloved sister. The thought of her has kept me going. I will find her — I must. I know that she is me — we are one and we will be together again. Nothing will stop me. She is my meaning and why I am here. She will save me from myself.

After a long time, he returned to the fire where Eve, still sitting, was reading from a small book he had not seen before.

'If this is my sister, I must save her from a life of servitude and bring us together — even if the remains of my family are only us. What was her situation?'

Eve had noticed Mya pausing in the corridors around Ko Tan and recalled a passing thought that there could be something more to Mya's relationship with her employer than merely pouring the drinks. However, she had no proof and did not want to upset Josefo more than he was.

'She's a maid — that is all.'

'Mmmm.' Josefo paused and the firelight danced in his eyes. 'What is that you are reading?'

Should she tell him about her father, her own loss, fear and journey of self-discovery that she had only just begun to discover for herself? She decided it was too early for those admissions. She did not know yet whether to trust him. Trust for her was something to be earned over time like watching watercress seeds grow into long slender fronds.

'It's just my diary — I read it at odd times.'

He let out a breath. 'We must sleep and awaken early in the morning. We still have many miles to go.'

18

Dottmar loved the house that Alex's father had owned. She loved the student gatherings in the days when she had yet to gain Alex's attention in any way other than as a friend. She had tagged along at first unsure of her surroundings and her status with the students from the wealthy landowning families in the city.

The first time she saw what was once the music room, she was enchanted, mesmerized by its size, light, warmth and charm. It felt to her like a scene out of Cinderella or some other fantasy world she had created for herself. Everything about this home was inviting. It welcomed her as a member of the family, one she was determined to join.

She thought back on herself in those days. How young she was. And beautiful too, she had been told. She looked at herself now in the mirror seeing only regret at what might have been if she had allowed it. The eyes no longer sparkling, the hair slightly dull, the limbs no longer as agile as they once were. It was age, certainly, but she knew it was more than that. Her youth was gone and her innocence had escaped long ago. Left with the here and now, she longed for the past.

That past was Alex.

She remembered only two things on that first day of school. Her heart hammering with fear and the blond-haired boy who had smiled at her as she had found a place at one of the desks. The fear would never disappear even though she learnt how to cope with it. She was not supposed to have gone to that school. The school for the rich. It was her mother who had noticed her outstanding abilities as a young child and insisted her father pursue the possibility of a scholarship with the principal. He had been impressed with her marks, even more with, for a girl of her age, her special areas of interest — communities, ecology and electronics.

Her background was not quite so pleasing for the Rangoon elite. Her parents had a small business selling vegetables to the market. They grew them on a plot at the end of the main street in the city. The tiny piece of land produced cabbages, pumpkin, potatoes and paw paw. Even the market stall holders were amazed at how such produce could emanate from a plot that size. While her parents did nothing but work, Dottmar engorged herself with learning. She consumed it like cooked cabbage and corned beef. Against protocol, the scholarship board decided to accept her.

While the other children were accompanied by their parents and *ayas* on that special first morning when reputations could be made or destroyed, Dottmar had to make her way to school alone. Her parents gave her their blessing but could not leave the ripening tomatoes at such a critical time. Her shoulders shook, she could hardly swallow as she walked into the classroom, keeping her eyes downcast until she glimpsed the blond boy's wide smile. Although dazzled, her shyness drove her to her seat with her nose embedded in the protective cover of her favorite book. She even remembered it: Lassie Come Home. She had loved the stories of animal heroes. It made her believe anything was possible. Alex had bolted to the first desk he saw and, dumping his books on the table, found himself sitting next to a small quiet girl with intense eyes.

His grin was met with a smile as he spread out his books and pens on the small space in front of him.

The last to arrive was a sooty-faced tousle-haired boy named Ko Tan. He sat himself down in the classroom's last remaining seat which happened to be opposite the blond-haired expat kid and the quiet vegetable seller's daughter. On this, the most important day of his son's life, Ko Tan's father had needed to conduct a last count of the geese in the yard before escorting him to class. He would never be late again.

The three young people found themselves in the extraordinary situation of becoming friends.

Dottmar remembered those days as if they had recently passed: the elite school, the passion for learning, the friendships she would never forget. She had longed to be part of the sophisticated families who seemed never to worry about money and who lived in the grand old mansions in the town. As she did not have such a family, she knew she would have to create one.

Alex with his fair skin and hair and easy personality was a magnet. She thought back and tried to distinguish which had come first, her ultimate goal or Alex. Her memory had fused them into one, but she knew she had always loved him.

She thought of Eve now and was amazed at her own strength for not blurting out the whole story to her. Ko Tan had been blunt.

'We will not lie — we just will not tell her the truth.' Dottmar had succeeded again in deceiving one she had grown to love.

19

The stirrings of a new life in one so young was like the flutter of a butterfly wing struggling at its cocoon. The woman child delighted in her growing belly, the belly button protruding indignantly through the silkiness of her billowing sari. She folded her hands over the taut skin as she had seen other mothers do in the plaza and patted the ripeness that was yet to drop from the vine. She marveled at the changes in her body, would never have believed such a tiny being could so distract her from everything. Its insistent kicking, rather than an irritant or pain, exhilarated her increasing anticipation of the day when she could let the chrysalis free to emerge into the world. She would be the guiding light for the new being — created her very self, born of her own womb enmeshed with the essence of him. They welcomed the baby into their Eden.

The long-awaited day arrived. She was shocked at the pain, at its suddenness and its longevity. A searing, tearing, never-ending agony the memory of which she thought would forever be burned in her mind. The birth was not an easy one — she did not need experience to know that. She longed for her husband's hand but as tradition would have it, he was barred from seeing his child's introduction to the world and from offering the hand of comfort to his young wife so desperately in need.

She felt light and heavy simultaneously and could see only a vision of white as her screams clouded her consciousness. She would not have minded if she had died. She reached out to the presence of white floating above her head, her hands almost touching the blue transparency, guiding her out of the noise and pain. An unimaginable tearing sensation brought her back to the room. She looked down to see a small round wet head slowly forcing itself into the light and the sight of this newly created being emerging into existence distracted her from the pain. Her baby was born — a wrinkly, red, angry piece of skin that was not easily pleased and demanded breath from the first instant.

Her next vision was the angry, red bundle being offered to her, placed on her breast for warmth and food.

Was this the creature that had been growing in her, nurturing the love and bonding she had felt in her bones? She looked at the small head, tiny eyes and grasping fingers and wondered where her love had gone. She held the creature to her breast and felt the first small springing of nectar that would continue to prolong its life. The gaping mouth grabbed her nipple with an intensity that scared her. How can this be? She looked up at the nurse with questioning eyes.

'Do I have to do this for long? I really do not like it!'

'Of course you silly girl — it is what mothers do. Do not worry, you will get used to it.'

Even then, with her child still wet from her own motherly juices, she knew she could not love this child as a mother should.

'Bring in the father!' bellowed the nurse. He burst in the door and saw her. He looked down at his little pink child and she saw a radiance in his eyes that she had never seen before. As he reached out to take the child in his arms, she saw the tears. Tears of joy for his new creation.

Once her child was gone, an emptiness overcame her which she could not describe. She had thought often about the child, where she was, what she looked like, how her life had turned out. She'd had one photograph in all those years. He had finally written, sent the letter and photo to the old familiar address in the hope of finding her. It was not a letter of love or regret or even bitterness. The words were full of sorrow at what she had done to them. He would never know how different it was for her.

20

Papa Chau Lap was 40 years old but looked older. The grey covered most of his head. He could thank his father for the fine mat of hair that had continued to sprout in his mature years. His face was weathered, not yet aged by years of life, but more by years in the sun and rain. He had strong upper arms made iron by toiling his ground and transporting the produce to the goods trucks. The sun was not welcome in the mountain plots that took years to cultivate the crop. As a boy, he had dreamed of owning his own farm. Most Chau Lap boys grew up to do just that, or join the army. He had done his military stint before his wife and children had entered his world: years that had claimed his youth, memories he made dim by choice. He often had bad dreams that chased him from the night into the day, dreams from which he was soon to discover he could never escape. Like the greying of his hair.

He and his brother, the Chau Lap boys, had been whisked away to serve their country. Plucked from a childhood of rice and bamboo and shoved into a world of live ammunition, lethal rocket launchers and death. He didn't allow himself to dwell on those events so he put them to one side, even now as he was leading the mountain community to what they thought would be a better life. He had had no choice; it was move them out or die.

The fact that he received a small endowment looked like some baksheesh to those whose imaginations had a single track. He needed that pittance to pay off any border patrols and to trade for food and essentials on the walk. He still had his son at his side and would do anything to protect him. He was the future.

As leader of the group there were always unpleasant duties to perform. He could forget most of them. But he could not forget Prasha. The young man had been walking with the group for days, was as weary as the rest and needing adrenalin. Prasha knew not to sample the crop, some of which had been processed to a point at which it was easier to trade. It was simply within his reach and he grabbed it. He prepared the lethal brew at camp on a rest break, found a silver spoon to heat the mixture over his campfire. It hit him instantly. Like a weapon forced into his temple taking away his consciousness.

Papa Chau Lap looked down at the man at his feet. He had seen young men do this despite the law of the mountains which was tacit but always understood. No mercy to those who break the sacred seal. No mercy to the opium thief.

Prasha began to moan and vomit white liquid. Papa knew what came next and he did not like it. But he was forced by the young men who insisted on living their lives against the rules.

It took all night to dig a hole wide and deep enough to hold a man standing. It was slow laborious work for his son, but Papa was certain he would do a good job.

Prasha had fallen in and out of consciousness as the night went on. Finally, the hole was ready. Papa gave the order to pick up Prasha and lower him into it. Camp was for three days, so Prasha's time in the hole could only be 72 hours. His screams were so fierce and frightening for the children that they had to stuff his mouth with rags and bind it with a cord. Unable to lie down but just lean against the walls, his insides were forced to contract and expand with a maximum of pain. Papa knew the entrenched addicts in his community and sympathized about the pain of withdrawal from the demon plant. But there was no alternative — an addict was no use to them or the farms. He had to be cured. He had done it so many times before. It was foolproof. But not this time.

The screams stopped. Nothing unusual in that — it would take two days and by the third day, coherency would return. But Prasha was different. After two days he had stopped screaming or making any noise. By the third day he was dead. He had half swallowed the gag and suffocated to death.

How did this happen — it had not happened before in his community. What had gone wrong? Papa Chau Lap questioned his son, went over events in his head and came up with nothing. He would have to bury the young man and tell his parents when they reached the lowlands. He would have much explaining to do.

They walked on through the jungle tracks on a well-worn path to their freedom. Only Papa Chau Lap knew this could never be the truth. Their futures were far from bright.

21

The miles and hours passed, sometimes with conversation about the mountains and Josefo's early life growing up surrounded by jungle. Eve thought that was a nice concept for all people — brought up feeling safe but with ever-present danger right on the doorstep of everyone's personal jungle.

'Do you dream?' she said aloud.

'Of course, I have many dreams. To increase my position in the party, to have many children.' He grinned that wide, white smile at her.

'No — I don't mean that sort of dream. The dream you have when you're asleep.'

He lost the smile. 'I do not have time for that.'

'We don't have much choice — the brain will do what it wants to do. And if it wants to give you a nightmare or a vision, it will do it. I sometimes have a recurring dream. You know, one that happens again and again. I often wonder what it means.' She told him of the dream she'd had many times. She was looking up from the depths of a dim and misty lake to see the underside of a boat on top of the water. A woman, dressed in black, was standing up in the small row boat flailing her arms hysterically and waving the oar. The woman lost her balance, falling into the water, sinking to the watery sand below. All in silence.

Eve had often wondered about this dream, one that had haunted her since childhood, one which kept returning. When had she last dreamt it and why did she think of it now?

'It's strange, isn't it, that I seem to be already drowned at the bottom of the lake but I'm concerned for the woman falling in above me. It's like I'm surviving in the water but she's not OK. I'm calm, but she's frantic. Although she has a boat, she still stuffs it up by falling in. And there's no sound.' She thought more logically about the dream. 'I wonder if it's me watching myself.'

Josefo looked quizzically at her, like a kindergarten student being taught calculus.

'I do not have dreams.'

'We all do. It's just that sometimes we don't remember them.' She turned to look at him. 'You can learn a lot from your dreams, Josefo.'

'You can learn a lot from listening and not talking so much,' he said.

22

The roads leading out of the mountains onto the border regions were well built but aging like the elderly men ruling the country. The road to one particular border region was unusual. This road began in the mountains and ended where two mountains met at a village. The village had, for hundreds of years, seen few inhabitants and survived on a subsistence farming culture with little more required of its inhabitants than finding food to feed the families and stock, making clothes and providing shelter. A simple existence. This society sustained itself for centuries with only five extended families and a few dwellings surrounding a central hut.

Some years before, a stranger found himself on the road where two mountains meet. San Wu was a young, ambitious man with ideas that would change the village forever. He loved the serenity of the mountains, and the village's secret location which made it difficult to find even with a map and lifelong knowledge of the area. Above all, he loved the raging river just beyond the valley. His eye for detail noticed that the area was perfect to defend. The high ground and secret location gave those who settled here the advantage while the river afforded even more protection. It was an ideal place for a group that did not want to be found and could defend itself if it were. As he approached the village, he summed up the requirements in his head — main house in lee of westward mountain slope, official headquarters across the valley, retractable bridge for narrow river crossing. Difficult but not insurmountable problems. There was nothing he couldn't do, he reminded himself. The oldest farmer emerged from his humble dwelling and greeted the stranger on the land that his family had owned and farmed for generations.

'Welcome young traveler – how can we help you?' said the old farmer.

The stranger was confident and walked up to the older man, his camouflage fatigues and ammunition belt strapped across his back. The farmer turned pale.

'You can start by gathering your family and possessions to prepare to move out by sundown. In the morning, I have 8,000 men arriving who will turn this haystack into a functioning military headquarters. You are, of course, welcome to stay under certain conditions.'

'On whose authority is this ordered? I will only obey our powerful President. No one else.'

'Thank you — yes. I have the President's blessing. Will you be staying or going?' said San Wu.

Most of the villagers had no choice but to stay. How could they prove what he said was true? At least, they thought, they could still farm their crops and keep their families safe. Some decided to leave, joining the long lines of trekking feet leaving the mountains for the lowlands and new farms. For those who stayed the house rules became harsh reality. It was a gradual realization that the simple though hard-working lives they had once taken for granted, were changed. There was a new world order and its leader was San Wu.

23

The unknown farmer made a difficult decision that day, one he would regret. His wife and children had left on a trek to the lowlands to begin a life free from the contamination of constant fear. He, however, would stay. He decided it would be only for a while so that he could help the remaining villagers retain what independence they still had. He would rejoin his family when the time was right. He could not know that he would never see his family again.

He was a savior for the remaining villagers, acting as a self-proclaimed guide in an existence that would be changed forever. As their mentor, he answered their questions, soothed their doubts and, however ignorant he was of the fact, he acted as a superlative marketing commander for the cause.

Each day he awoke to new noise and the sound of marching feet, feet that eventually would take over the life blood of the village he had known as a quiet farming community since he was a baby.

There were crops being farmed, the usual poppy on the high ground was yielding higher and higher quantities as all available land was taken. Poppies had been farmed in these mountains for hundreds of years but the farmer couldn't remember or understand why their relentless pursuit was so frenetic. It was relaxing to take some syrup once in a while (if you dared) and many of the farmers had grown up on the secret passion of the poppy. But the popularity of the plant astounded him. Thousands of small fields of half an acre to an acre were being cleared all around the township and close to the border country. San Wu had engaged slash and burn parties — experts in land clearing who had inherited their skills from their traditional farming families.

What was once grown on this land was used to feed his family and the farmer was happy with the subsistence culture of his and the few other families in the town. The main product was to be a strange green gum that was scraped off the poppy head and placed in large sacks. This gum was unaffected by transport delays, heat or rain unlike vegetables and fruit crops. It was invincible and was treated like gold. Anyone even contemplating taking a spoonful for later was pitted. The farmer had witnessed this practice. Not many men had survived six months in the pit as punishment for a lick of the spoon. It was little deterrent for those whose bodies had become used to the elixir. The farmer could not see the value in this commodity. It only caused misery and death and yet the village grew from the five families to a sprawling town of 20,000 people in a mere ten years.

The profits from the pretty poppy never stopped.

The young and ambitious military man in camouflage pants had become the great leader San Wu. At first, he could be seen walking all over the village, visiting the barracks to call on the men, taking a small group with him to the mountains to check on the plots close by. His entourage had grown over the years until he had finally put another young man in charge and had slowly disappeared from the public eye.

The farmer and San Wu had developed a friendship of a kind and at first, after his initial shocking actions that transformed his village into a mutation, had grown to respect him and his ideals. He was forging a freedom party in opposition to the government. Wasn't this what his country needed? To free the people from moral and physical servitude and to profess independence in word and action?

Later it became apparent to the farmer that San Wu had other motivations.

The village's humble shacks and animal pens soon gave way to modern compounds, shops and accommodation for the growing army that was giving the town a new identity. He could see a new structure being erected on the hill and could identify where the masonry and logs had been delivered. One morning, he decided to investigate the progress of this structure and walked to the embankment overlooking the lowlands and the river which was filling its banks. The building was almost complete. It was something he had never seen before. The double doors formed a grand entry to a three-storey structure which seemed to be supported by several vertical pillars. As he approached the huge opening, he entered an amazing hall with space for ten fields of crops and as high as the sky. The farmer couldn't work out what would be the purpose of such a building. There were no rooms for beds, no pens for animals, not even a fountain for good luck. He was only to know much later that the building was to be used for bartering over chips, and winning and losing large amounts of cash. The town had its own casino.

The farmer had never seen a casino before and didn't understand the concept of bartering for money. Money was not a useful commodity in the early years. It was only later in his life that he had seen the greed and hunger produced by the flimsy paper. He could understand bartering and trading in furs, skins and vegetable goods. But the trade of money for money was beyond his comprehension.

'We need money to buy what we need,' explained San Wu.

'We have never needed supplies — we have always supplied ourselves with what we need. Now we ship them in. It is because of this casino!'

'Hah! The casino is nothing. Wait till you see my bowling alley — but that will be only for me!'

The farmer looked away from the grinning man who was at the peak of his confidence. He was laughing and standing with his legs wide apart, with his hands on his hips. How he had changed from the insecure young man in military fatigues who had come on reconnaissance to the village.

San Wu went on to explain his first experience of bowling and how much pleasure it had given him.

'I deserve this,' he muttered and turned toward his headquarters at the top of the hill. The farmer watched him striding up the hill, waving and gesticulating to himself, his wide mouth emitting throaty guffaws.

It was the last time the farmer saw San Wu so close. San Wu began to distance himself from the townspeople and while he had once been a leader in touch with his men, he now spurned their company and rarely left his homestead on the hill. Once in a while the farmer would wake in the night and hear a faint thud followed by the jubilant cry of a chorus of voices. He would come to recognize this sound of a bowling ball hitting the pin. Once he heard the last cry, sleep beckoned once more.

*

San Wu knew he was destined to be a fighter. His father was the chieftain of a highlands village and he and his six brothers were taught early the skills of weaponry and self-defense. Recruited into the rebel army at 16, San Wu climbed the ranks by diligence and fortitude. He had met the English Tiger, Raoul, who had been impressed with his bravery and confidence in the face of any obstacle. San Wu's people were used to fighting battles — they were not afraid of death. Raoul welcomed him into the party and gave him control until Alex was ready to take over.

His father had been one of the original group that Raoul had trusted with his secret. The young son had been initiated at an early age and thought he was destined to be the leader. He believed he would achieve far more than the Tiger ever had. The Tiger had not been brought up in civil war, had not been taught to fight with his hands and outwit his enemies with jungle survival tactics. These were skills learnt only in the mountains by other fighters and those accustomed to death.

The old farmer's background was not unlike San Wu's life in the mountains — training in weaponry, sword handling and patrolling in the jungle. But the farmer had, after his early training, preferred a life of producing crops from the ground and raising children. That life would soon change.

24

Mya walked down the corridor of the house and let herself out the front door. The evening was unusually moonlit, there was not a cloud to dim the luminescence. The light cast by the moon allowed her to follow the path from the house through the courtyard and the long line of banyan trees onto the main road. From here it was not a long walk down a gradient to the town. She was a fast walker and knew the quickest route through some private alleys to avoid the busy roads. At this time of night there were still a few cars on the road but not the chaotic gridlock to be seen at noon. She had chosen the quietest part of the night — not yet morning when the world was awakening.

She had left her side of the bed without waking Ko Tan. He was a heavy sleeper and knew that she often had to get up in the night. She knew he would be unaware of how long she had been gone. Before she'd left him, she had found his money clip on the dressing table and taken most of his paper money. Now away from the house and in a private laneway behind one of the grand old homes of Rangoon, she dived into the secret place in her sarong and counted the cash — 51,700 kyat — about US$50. They normally only accepted US dollars but today they would have to take local kyat. She was confident of her persuasive abilities with men. And they were always men who did the deals. She smiled to herself at being so lucky with the amount this evening. Ko Tan didn't normally carry that much on him. He would notice but would say nothing.

She moved adeptly through the narrow streets until she found herself in the town's main square. There were a few people around — some she recognized but most were beggars and homeless souls struggling to find a vacant space in which to get some rest.

She slowed down as she entered the square where the beggars and street people were not to be trusted. Looking in front and behind she knew only too well the risks of being caught off guard. Long ago in another lifetime in a square not so different from this one, she had spent a night discovering the frightening reality of desperate men with a bloodlust for money. Bleeding and betrayed she had made her way back to unwelcoming lodgings bereft of money, nectar and her dignity. She had vowed never to let that happen again.

She moved swiftly to the nearest wall and followed its length to an archway. A shadow moved in front of her. Mya could not know this was the same archway where Abau had been killed and Eve taken.

She caught the attention of the figure in the shadows.

'Have you got the money?' he hissed.

'Yes it is all here — US$50 — in kyat. Count it.'

He grabbed the bundle of notes she had pulled from her pocket, licked his fingers and started counting.

He pushed a small wad of something covered in plastic. She was surprised he didn't even blink at the kyat. It was not a treasured currency.

'That is all there is for a while. I will be in touch.'

'What do you mean a while? How long? When will you be back?'

The man and his shadow were gone.

Mya hid the package in a pocket and hurried to a protected wall where she had a 360-degree view of the square. She knew she couldn't be seen so she pulled out the package to check the contents. She unwrapped the bundle. It held some dark grey sticky paste weighing, she calculated, about 20 mg. With the treatment, it would last two days maybe three. Not enough. She usually had a week's supply with that amount. She knew the man in the shadows had given her far less than before for the same price but he was gone so quickly. She had to get more.

She put the package away and looked around the square. Most of the stragglers seemed to have found a place to store their meagre belongings and get some sleep. At the end of the square, she could see a man, upright with an unusual bearing. As she drew closer, she thought he had a clean face and clothes. He seemed familiar to her. She made her way toward him, slowly swaying her hips in an exaggerated style and putting her head on one side. She undid the buttons on her *yinzi* revealing the plump skin of her cleavage and raised her sarong as if to miss a puddle that would dirty the fabric. Her eyes were keenly fixed on him as she made her way across the street. She could see he had noticed her and he was watching as she approached. He didn't waver his gaze or move but leant up against the wall and waited. Her heart pounded. She hadn't done this for a long time but her body needed nectar and he was her opportunity.

History had told her most men didn't like mystery. This type of man anyway. Ko Tan was different. He had treated her well and given her feelings she had never known existed. She put him out of her mind as she found herself leaning into the man's shoulder, grasping his hand and placing it on the warm flesh beneath the thin fabric of her *yinzi*. She guessed he was a merchant from one of the local shops possibly out getting some air or having a cigarette after a busy night. She could smell smoke on his clothes. He didn't pull his hand away, no surprise in that. And yet, he did nothing more than watch her with keen black eyes.

'How much would you like?' He didn't whisper but his voice was not loud.

'I need 520,000 kyat.' This was a large amount of money — almost US$500 — but she always aimed high — then there was room for bargaining.

'That is a lot of money for a little girl. What do you want it for?' She had never been asked this before. Most men just paid up or gave what they chose.

'My father is sick and I need to get him some medicine urgently.'

'Is this always the way you get your father medicine?'

'It is the quick way.' She had the words out before she could stop herself. She was aware that this man was not usual, something about him puzzled her.

'There was a young girl down here the other night disturbing people wanting just to sleep — coming up to men like you are doing now. Was that you, maybe?'

'No! No I have just decided tonight — I am desperate!'

'Have you done this sort of thing before?' His hand was still on her flesh, unmoving.

'N...' She hesitated and remembered that Ko Tan had told her about new security in the town. Her heart started to pound again and she slowly pulled away from him, crouching low and backing away.

'I can give you 5,000 kyat — but that is all.' He put

his now free hand into his top pocket to pull out what she expected to be kyat paper notes. She was not impressed by this amount of money but it would provide two or three hits, she thought.

As he watched her expectant face, his eyes were smiling. He drew out something from his wallet, something that glistened metallic in the moonlight and was oval encased in a leather pouch.

'I am off duty but you are on my turf, little girl. Do you want the money or not?'

25

E ve was still in the twilight zone between sleep
and wakefulness when she sensed a change in
the environment. She sat up in her sleeping bag
and felt a chill in the air very different from the usual
enveloping heat of the city. Up in the mountains it was
cooler. Her clothes were damp from sweat at the end of
the day but the nights were fresh. It was first light and
she could see Josefo packing the jeep for the next leg of
the journey. They were only a day from the border town
where they would head north to San Wu's village, Josefo
had told her. She had sensed someone approaching and
a feeling of anxiety began to brew in her bones. She
shivered like a child.

'Josefo — there's someone coming. What's
happening?' She called out to him as he busied himself
in the campsite.

'I have heard it too. Get ready to leave. We need to
find more protection behind those boulders.' He pointed
to a copse of trees surrounding very large exposed rocks
that looked as if they had been broken from the ridge
and left orphaned at the bottom of the ravine.

They packed hastily and moved the jeep behind the
trees. They waited. It was not long before a young man
appeared in the clearing, carrying a weapon which

appeared to be an old rifle. He stopped by the ashes of last night's fire, kicked the dirt and surveyed the area. He walked around the perimeter, then turned as another older man appeared behind him.

'This looks good, Papa, but someone has been here not long before us. Do you think we should stay or move on to a safer harbor?'

'The women need to rest. Just do your best at protecting our perimeter. That is all we can do.'

The older man retreated from where he had come. Soon he returned leading a line of people into the small clearing. There were old and young women, children and young people. People of all ages with one thing in common. They dragged their feet in search of rest, wore dirt from head to toe and carried large sacks fastened to their backs with thick ropes. They were pack animals bundled with a heaviness like mud in the wet.

One of the women placed an old cloth on the ground. She placed on it a child of about four. She laid the child carefully on the cloth and gently wiped his dust-streaked face with a damp rag. The child began to cough, turned over clutching his knees and lowered his head into his chest. His cough slowly subsided while other mothers did the same with their children in all parts of the camp. Eve guessed there were thirty people in this dirty bedraggled group.

The older man who had first entered the clearing was tending to each of the families who had started to settle themselves into the space. He went from one to the next offering his help with the children and levelling the land if it was rough. Once he had seen to everyone, he stood up, stretched and turned to the younger man who had kept a small space for him near a tree. He placed himself next to the younger man, folded his arms and rested his head on the trunk.

'I know who these people are — we must move on,' Josefo whispered to Eve.

'Who are they?'

'They are moving south to set up farms. They are no danger to us. We must continue.'

'I'd like to speak to that older man. He looks kind. I want to know what's going on. Perhaps we can help them?'

'No! You must not speak to these local people. My orders are to take you to San Wu, and that is what I will do. You will speak to no one.'

Eve didn't wait for a response and before Josefo could stop her she was moving towards the leader of the bedraggled group.

Papa Chau Lap was almost asleep when he heard his son rising next to him. He opened his eyes to see someone approaching — unarmed and female. He blinked a few times, thinking he may be having a psychotic dream, but rather than disappear, she drew closer. She stopped in front of him.

'Um, hello, excuse me,' Eve started. She paused and when there was no response, she continued. 'I – we saw you. I didn't want to scare you. My name is Eve. Are you alright?' As she spoke she turned around to see Josefo approaching the group, weapon in hand.

Papa Chau Lap rose to meet this threat to his group. At the same time his son had assumed the stance of a trained fighter — rifle at eye level and cocked. A local with a weapon was not to be ignored. Eve stopped, put her hands up and said: 'Please, I just wanted to talk to you. I have no weapon.' Her heart was beating fast. One hyperactive trigger finger and she could be hit, worse than killed, wounded. She pictured herself having to walk the rest of the way with a gangrenous leg, limping across jagged rocks, Josefo half carrying her fragile frame. The younger man, initially spooked, now stopped moving forward and seemed to calm. He looked at the older man.

'Josefo — please no! I just want to talk ...' Josefo and Papa's son lowered their rifles to the ground, skittish as cats and just as unpredictable. Josefo did not take his eyes off the younger man. Papa Chau Lap looked straight at Eve.

'Do you speak English?' she asked.

'Some. I am Papa Chau Lap — you can call me Papa.'

*

'People do not stop and talk. I can tell you our story.' Eve nodded. His son had moved away while Josefo stayed close enough to hear the conversation but kept his distance.

They were both offered a weak tea and some wheaten biscuits. Josefo drank the tea but refused the biscuits. Papa was willing to talk. He wondered who she was, why she was here and whether he should trust her with his story. He decided to tell her the truth about the journey of his people, what they had left and what they would find. There was something about this woman he sensed was not dangerous to him. He told her everything — how they had to leave their livelihoods with a promise for a great future, the loss of fifty lives on their journey and the reality of what was to come. He had not shared this with his own people.

Eve kept her eyes on his throughout his story, not distracted, not interrupting, just nodding occasionally. He could not remember the last time he had shared a conversation with someone who had drunk in his every word. It was a strange but exhilarating feeling. When he finished, he took a large sip of his third mug of tea and leant back, relaxing against the bark of the tree. After sipping his tea, he looked up from his mug and was surprised to see that she had wet cheeks. He looked to her colleague and saw that the blood had drained from his face.

There was silence while Papa waited for her to respond.

Eve closed her eyes and bowed her head for a moment. She looked at him again.

'I come from Australia where we can do what we want when we want. If we don't break the law, we have a very free life. It doesn't seem to be the same here. Is no one doing anything about it? Can anything be done?'

No one had asked Papa Chau Lap this question before. Most of his tribe lived day to day and endured what happened to them with little question. There was no point in fighting an army of 8,000 men — it was safer to go along with their wishes. Questions of reason, options, alternatives and possible transformation of the end result were issues he had not faced in a long time.

'I do not know how to answer, Eve. I have thought long about it. Many have died trying to change things. Some things cannot be changed. In order to survive, one has to obey. The main problem is the opium.' Papa looked down at his hands. 'It is this plant, it is too hardy, long-lasting, hard to kill, easy to transport — unlike any other plant we have in this country.'

'What will it take to solve the problem?'

'If you could discover a plant that does all these things but heals instead of destroys, we may be able to get somewhere!' He turned to his son with a laugh. 'Impossible!'

'I am on my way to see San Wu — do you know who he is? We will be at his camp in two days. I can talk to him about your problem. If he is anything like Josefo says, I may be able to get him to help us.'

Papa Chau Lap laughed.

'You must be joking! No one can talk San Wu around — least of all a white woman who has no idea about our culture!' Papa muttered under his breath to his son who guffawed. 'What has this so-called guide been telling you?' He stood up now and moved over to where Josefo was squatting. He looked down at the younger man.

'Tell me. Have you met the man you admire so much, the biggest opium addict of all?'

Josefo's face drained of blood, and left his dark skin the color of ashes.

'I did not think so — very few have and certainly none of your age, I think.'

Eve turned to face Josefo.

'Josefo? Why did you tell me so many stories about him and his ideals, his values, the promise of good for his people?' Eve stood up and dusted herself off. 'I was starting to trust you.'

'Do not be too hard on him, Eve,' Papa said. 'It is very much the way — when we respect someone, we must not lose face by revealing what we do not know! It sounds strange, but it is the way of our culture. I can tell this boy admires you.'

Josefo's face went from ashen to bougainvillea red. This time he could not stay seated. He stood up and faced Papa Chau Lap.

'I have met San Wu. It happens to be a long time ago — when I was just past a child. He trained me but I have not been able to see him for a long time.' He looked at Eve. 'I was not lying. My memory is strong. And I know he wants me to be 2IC. He is not opium addict.'

'Be careful, Josefo. Do not believe what you hear on the opium vine. Even from San Wu himself, I would not trust this news. Think about what he wants — not what you want. Guard against this man.'

Eve started to feel the beginnings of a heaving chest and dry mouth.

'Josefo, will it be safe to see him?'

'Do not ever count on safety, Eve.' Papa looked over at Josefo who had gathered his weapon and ammunition in a bundle on his back.

'Do not worry. It is time we started moving again.'

'But Papa, I would like to meet you again. You can leave a message for me at the old house at One Grevillea Drive in the city. Please find me.'

The small, tired group huddled together to get as much comfort as they could. Papa saw the white woman leaving and hoped he would meet her again.

26

Eve had remembered their last meeting, like so many before, devoid of intimacy and connection. She would visit her father in his small, modest house away from the bustle of life to take a meal or watch television together. Standing at the kitchen bench, he would spend what seemed like hours cutting and chopping, pounding and scraping, loud sounds emanating from the small room until he would finally emerge with a humble repast of chops and mash or baked beans on toast.

She wondered how he had managed to survive all these years with no woman at his side. He would talk about the weather, his work at the office or ask her about her plants, her research and the PhD. Never more than that. Never about Roger or babies. Nothing about the past, or the future. It had become his method. She came to believe it was his way of avoiding anything unpleasant in his own life or others. Pain was to be avoided. Voided. Life equals no pain. Yet pain was his life. Under his mask of contentment she knew there lay something — dissatisfaction, exhaustion, lost motivation. Somewhere there must have been a life she had missed.

He had opened the door to her on that last time before his death, a slow grey smile on his face with a warmth in his eyes she had seen diminish slowly throughout her life. An almost imperceptible quieting, her father had become silent unless pushed for more. This silence pervaded the room while he offered her a chair and tea to share.

The room was immaculate — as always. Sparsely furnished with nothing newer than 20 years old, he had a minimalist taste that defied any culture. There was nothing of his past to show what sort of life he had led. There were photographs of Eve but no other family.

'I never had many photos of your mother,' he would say when she asked him why they were only of Eve. 'I just don't have any of her — oh, except this one.' He had forced himself out of the chair and reached into a shelf above the bookcase, carefully pulling something out of a book. He brought it to Eve. She studied the photo which showed the slim figures of a man and a woman. The woman was holding a baby. The man, clearly Alex, was beaming at the camera above the woman's head which was fully obscured as she looked into her baby's eyes away from the camera. They appeared to be on a verandah, cane chairs and green fronds from a palm crawled into the corner of the photograph.

All Eve could make out of her mother was a slim frame and curly dark hair. They looked happy. It didn't feel like Australia.

Alex had said it was their first holiday together and their last — in tropical Broome to the north of the state. The furthest either of them had travelled, he'd said.

Eve loved the photo and made her father frame it and display it on the bookshelf but once she had left, he had placed it in a drawer.

'Dad — you seem withdrawn these days and pale. Is there anything wrong? You know I worry about you?' She didn't often get so intimate with him but she had noticed him being more withdrawn than usual and not asking as many questions — even if it was only about the latest television show or the cricket.

'No Eve — I'm alright. Haven't had a sick day in my life. You should be proud of me. I'll last till I'm a hundred.'

'Well, I mean in yourself not necessarily your health. How are you in yourself?'

He stopped briefly and looked at her.

'Ah, that's for me to know and you to find out,' he chuckled, bringing over her cup of tea. 'Anyway, tell me about your research projects. How is the new genus coming — or is that genius?' He chuckled again at his own wit and then receded into the chair as she gave him a potted history of what she chose to tell him about her work.

'By the way, love. Why is it that you have to work in people's gardens to get research money — you should be getting government funding, surely?'

She hadn't wanted to go into her recent change of circumstance from PhD horticulture student to gardener to the elderly. She wasn't yet ready to share the moment the ground gave way beneath her feet. That was an interesting analogy, she thought, as her life and work was the earth. She'd managed to hide many things from her father, as most daughters are able. She figured if he didn't ask, she didn't tell. They were both happy with selective sharing.

Once tea was consumed, he was transfixed by the moving images on the television and while including her in the life on the screen, she felt that creating a bond by sharing television viewings was long beyond her. He didn't make it easy.

'Dad — did you ever regret not having more children? How come you only had one?'

'I've told you, Eve. Your mother couldn't have any more and then she died. But I was always more than happy with my little Eve.' He reached out his hand to touch hers briefly and then withdrew it.

'Really? You never seemed especially happy in my memory. You always seemed stressed or preoccupied.' She was going cutting edge.

'It's not easy being a single father for most of a child's upbringing. And I had to work as well. It was difficult.'

She struggled to understand how hard it had been for him shuffling paper from one side of a desk to another which would then be transported to another set of clerical workers moving the same bit of paper across their desks. She was sure it hadn't challenged him but she knew she couldn't judge him for it. His brain was capable of more. He spoke to her sometimes of world events, historical facts and displayed a memory that she recognized was as unusual as her own. His pencil sketches were perfect and he had a gift for military tactics displayed during their early chess games. But he had chosen an ordinary life and abandoned those rich conversations long ago. She thought there was just so much more he could have done.

'How's Roger?' He asked, eyes glued to the screen. It was India versus Australia.

What could she answer? Tell the truth or protect him from the facts? Would protecting him serve a purpose? As the offspring she sometimes wondered why she needed to protect the parent. Wasn't that the parent's job, for life?

'He's leaving me, Dad. He's found another woman

who's having his baby.'

He averted his gaze from the cricket score and looked at her.

'I'm sorry, sweetie — I didn't realize. How are you taking it?'

'My husband has impregnated another woman who is now carrying the child he's wanted for the last eight years so I suppose I should be happy for him — them. He's got what he's always wanted.'

'But Eve — you were right to stand your ground on that with him.' She felt supported at last.

'Though I must say, if you'd had a child you would have experienced the most fundamental love and spiritual event that can ever happen to a woman and her husband.'

Her heart slid back to earth with a thud.

'But it's always up to the woman in the end. You've done the right thing. Don't worry about it. It's for the best. Someone else will come along.'

It was like her father to brush emotion off like a feather. And like a feather he would crush it to insignificance. Couldn't he see she was distraught, betrayed, hurt even if she didn't choose to openly share it with him? He must have some intuition.

He was thumping his knee at the latest score of play and grinning. That grin behind vacant, grey eyes.

'What did it feel like when you lost mum? Were you upset — what did you do when you had a child to support on your own?'

He looked away from the television but not at Eve. He was looking at a more distant place — one that she hadn't seen or been invited to enter.

'It was the worst day of my life. For the universe or God to choose between you both was an impossible choice. To lose her like that broke my heart, Eve. But I had you to sustain me. I so needed your love as a child — and you were so affectionate — you made up for all that past hurt. Your mother couldn't help it.'

It was interesting the way he talked now, never mentioning her death in the accident but just leaving Eve to remember the story he had told her for as long as she could remember. But he did not say the words — it was as if she hadn't physically died but just in his heart.

'Did it seem like I missed my mother at all as a young child?'

'Why all these questions, Eve — what's going on? Just because Roger has chosen a different direction from you doesn't mean you have to change yours.'

'Dad — Alex — why can you never sustain a conversation for longer than five minutes about my mother? Or of your past that I know so little about.'

'I've told you the interesting bits and about your mother — that should be enough. Your own life is far more interesting than mine ever was.' He rested back in his chair, his face pale and his hands slightly shaking.

'Are you alright, Dad? You don't look too good.'

'I just need a little rest before dinner, sweetie — if you don't mind I need to lie down. Can you see yourself out and push in the lock? I'll call you tomorrow.' And conversation ended. Just like his life the following day.

*

He watched her leave that last time and though he didn't know he would never see her again, he felt a deep sadness for her and the life he had chosen to give her. Without a mother's love, how could a child really develop into a woman capable of rearing and loving a child of her own? It was no wonder the girl had never had maternal feelings. He had made her too self-sufficient or, at least, caused her to be by his own distant nature. He knew it in himself, couldn't deny it. He felt the absence he had created for her and her desperate independence that insisted on making her live a life she hadn't chosen. But what were his choices? Certainly death — or life? He had chosen life. Or had he? Eve would probably think he hadn't chosen life but something in between life and death that only he could experience. A kind of half-life. It was adequate for his needs. He had never wanted to relive the crazy world he'd come from, a world so many miles away from the searing heat and red dust of Australia. It had taken him a long time to get used to this new land. It was so different and even in those days, with his skills, it was almost impossible for a migrant to get decent work for real money. It had been a struggle, something Eve would never understand.

27

Something made Ko Tan stir and he woke up from a restless sleep. Instinctively, he reached out to feel for Mya and was disappointed to find she was not in the bed beside him. He knew she had left him in search of her life saver, the sweetness that would make her sleep. He felt he could only help her by providing the very thing he knew would one day destroy her. At least he knew she was under his control, he was feeding her the juice, or at least providing a safe means by which to obtain it. It was a small price to pay. He was not a poor man and it was a meagre amount each month to him but a fortune for her. Recently he had begun to question his own generosity if he could call it that. Even with his handouts, she had been taking money from his wallet, expecting him not to notice and certainly not to face her with it. She was right — he would never do that. But more often she was gone in the night. He didn't know where and assumed that she was placing herself in some danger or, at the very least, a highly risky situation. He knew she had been used to that in the past but his goal had been to make her welcome in his home and rid her of the demon that made her a wretched thief — and worse.

He opened his eyes to follow the line of his arm and

feel the empty space next to him. He could sense she was no longer in the room but she had not been gone long, he knew that. The space where she slept was still warm from her flesh.

He forced himself from his comfortable position and rolled to one side as he contemplated getting up. As he pondered he could hear some movement in the corridor outside his room and made himself get to his feet and go to the door.

As he opened it he half expected to see Mya, smiling as if nothing had happened making her way to bed. Instead he came face to face with his wife, Dottmar.

'Looking for your girlfriend? She was seen walking the streets, you foolish man!' Dottmar spat these words at the man she had once loved.

'Thank you for pointing that out to me, my dear. I am sure she will be back soon.'

'Why do you bother, Ko Tan? What is this hold she has over you? You are the age her father would be now — if she ever knew who he was!'

Ko Tan did not oblige her with an answer, lowered his head and retreated into his room. Dottmar was left in the corridor. He knew she could not face him with the real question constantly on her lips: 'What happened to what we had?' He had given her the answer.

He turned toward his dressing table and looked in the mirror. He had the distinguished grey hair young women often found attractive and older women wanted to dye. His face was still strong and his eyes bright. There were certainly lines in his skin but he assured himself they were lines of experience and maturity. He wanted to defy age. He remembered once looking into this very mirror with Dottmar at his side on their wedding night all those years ago. She had been beautiful — she still was if he chose to notice. He didn't look into her eyes any more. But he remembered her as a young woman. The day she started school and Alex and he had vied for her attention. Attention that Alex always won. When Ko Tan had eventually won her over, when there was no more challenge, she succumbed to his charms and allowed him to have her first as a lover then as a wife. He remembered the feeling of excitement and exhilaration as he watched her making her way down the aisle, the most magnificent bride he had ever seen. And she was his! When they were together in this room on their wedding night, he engulfed himself in her, unaware of anything else. It was a bliss that he could still remember but he had to admit, was a struggle to bring to the surface.

He couldn't tell when it had started to disintegrate — he didn't choose to remember. These things just happened to everyone after a period of time. They had developed an understanding and then Mya came into his world like a newly born calf, struggling to stand on her feet. He no longer felt like an old man, used up and past it. He was rejuvenated by her very youth climbing the ladder to heaven on earth. She was his salvation in a sea of ordinariness. From the moment he first saw her — not much more than a child — to now, he had loved her with an intensity he had never thought possible.

Dottmar had been the strong one in their marriage; the woman who nurtured and protected him. Now he could be the protector of someone else and feel indispensable. He had only one concern — the drugs or the nectar as she liked to call it. It had surrounded his whole life but he had never been so close to its lethal effects as he had with Mya. He was shocked at first but like most things, after he began to get used to the idea, he became more tolerant and understanding of her needs — her constant demands. But it was always his choice when he gave her money — always, that is, until tonight.

She had not stolen from him for a long time. He had always given freely and with no attachments. Now it was different. He had acted out of love, he told himself. He wanted to help her, to save her from herself and her self-destructive personality. It was only when he had discovered her for the first time begging, crawling, grasping at him like a dog pleading for help, nectar, money — anything to stop her insides from eating her away. He had seen desperate people before but usually they were desperately poor, lonely, frightened — not like this. She was something more — ready to do anything for a shot of calming fluid that would lift her to dizzy paroxysms of pleasure that would last merely minutes. After the desperation came the soliloquy of a breath, the miasma of her essence turned into love at a touch. He didn't want her like this — she was neither of these people but more and more she was becoming something he did not recognize. He needed to stop her — even just to save himself from the fear of her inevitable death.

He thought she wouldn't notice the smaller amounts of money he gave her or how he forgot to put money in her room each week. She would ask for it but he continued to make excuses and would offer to buy her food, sarongs and kohl pencil whenever he went to town.

She could have everything she wanted as long as she didn't inject it into her body. He had not anticipated the change in her. One minute she became sullen and mute then the next manically happy, trying to please his every mood so he would succumb and give her what she wanted. He proved stronger than he would ever have thought as she turned into a thief and a liar to get her way.

But he still loved her. Different from the way he had once loved Dottmar. Beautiful Dottmar, smart, strong, ambitious Dottmar who had also become someone he did not recognize. She had once been young, gentle, sweet and now — he felt no connection. He knew she felt the same way. They had ended any real relationship years ago. The boys, rather than drawing them closer, had forced them further apart.

Ko Tan had followed Mya only once before and had vowed never to do it again. She had been surprised at seeing him, but then angry at having to reveal her secret. He didn't like what he found — but he noticed disappointment getting less each time.

He knew she couldn't have gone far and made an impetuous decision. He would go into town. She would either be in the main square or somewhere else he didn't want to think about.

He walked the path through the moonlight Mya had followed only a short time earlier. Through the alleys down the main hill over the cobbled stone pavements and steps, he chased the moon.

When he came to the town square, there were very few people visible. Those who dotted the periphery of the square were people he did not want to meet again. He had encountered such people throughout this life but found them contemptible failures, unable to abate the flow of opposing forces destroying their lives. There were beggars, street people with no bed to call their own, city scum who had fallen between the cracks of respectable society. He pushed away the thought that Mya may still fall into the category she had once inhabited. He yearned to see her, yet dreaded it too. He knew only too well what the outcome would be.

He moved around the square studying each face as he went. Most had covered or filthy faces, impossible to recognize. After walking around for some time, he began to feel a lessening anxiety and leant against a street wall that led to a row of shops. Just as he reached into his coat pocket to draw out a cigarette, a neatly dressed man approached him.

'Match, sir?' He offered a lit match and Ko Tan cupped his hands around the burning flame to ignite the cylinder he would soon inhale.

'You looking for someone in particular — or just looking ...?' The man turned his mouth up at the edge which formed a rather cocky smirk that Ko Tan did not take to.

'Why is that your business?'

'Because I know a young woman you may want to meet. She has been naughty. I believe it is about money.' Again he smirked and started walking toward a building which glowed with light from a small window.

Ko Tan had the impression the man wanted him to follow. He walked behind the man, through a corridor to the room with the small window. To his left and sitting disheveled behind an iron grating, was Mya. He could see she had been crying but she appeared to have calmed herself and now had the look of a wilting plant left without water on a blisteringly hot day. When she saw Ko Tan she jumped to her feet and ran to the bars that separated her from her protector.

'Ko Tan! I willed you to come!' She clung tightly to the bars smiling up at him.

'How much is the bail?' Ko Tan had experience enough to know not to ask for reasons or to expect any logical responses.

'It is 500 US dollar,' the man said smiling slightly to Mya as he said it. She blanched and turned away from the bars to face the wall. Ko Tan looked back at the man and handed over the money.

'This means a lot to Mya, I trust,' he said as he moved over to the grill and turned the key in the lock.

Mya held herself and walked out of the cell toward Ko Tan not looking back at the man.

Ko Tan had been through similar experiences with Mya over the few years they had been together. She said she would never do it again, and he forgave her. He knew she would lie and do it again but there was something about her smile and the expression of vulnerability in her eyes that he could not deny.

'I will make it up to you Ko Tan — I'll be good and pay back the money. I just want to be good to you, Ko Tan,' Mya smiled up at him adjusting herself and her clothes.

'Come home now, Mya — we need our sleep.'

28

Eve realized she had been sitting in the passenger seat for some time. She had become so tied up in her recollections that she had lost all awareness of her surroundings. She resurfaced with a start, her head pounding and her body aching. Josefo had been driving all this time, without interruption.

'How's the driving? You OK? I can drive for a while if you want,' she looked in his direction. 'Even though you've kidnapped me.'

'I could not let a woman drive — not in this country. Anything might happen!' He didn't appear to be joking, but she was too tired to confront his chauvinism and not in the mood for any debate.

'Suit yourself — I'm going to try to sleep some more.'

'Well do not get too comfortable — we are not very far from the border. Then we walk.'

'What do you mean, walk? I thought we could drive directly into the settlement?' The idea of walking was sinking in.

'It is impossible. The road ends at a huge mountain, more track, then we cross a bridge. The settlement is just over the bridge.'

'How far — how long?' She didn't want to know.

'Not long.' From what she had learned of this man's expressions, this could mean anything. As there appeared to be nothing she could do about it, she relaxed back into the seat and slept for as long as she could, feeling the road's every rock and ditch against the small of her back.

*

Josefo looked at Eve and realized he had never met a woman like her. He had met strong women before but they were tough: jungle or street smart and less than appealing. Yet though they were tough, he didn't let their toughness get in the way of a good night in. He found he could woo any woman he chose. There was something about him that charmed them without his trying very hard. He had learned of his special skill in his early years when he could defy his mother with no reproach. It was only later he learned that he could use this skill with women of his own age for a much more pleasurable outcome.

The woman who was sitting in the passenger seat, eyes shut, lashes lowered and soft body relaxed against the tumble of the jeep's movement, was tough, but in a subtle way. On first sight, her appearance was not remarkable — dull, blondish, straggly hair like ironed cotton threads at shoulder length, freshness of face and nondescript clothes with strange shoes. But he had come to like the understated way she communicated. There was no pretense, none of the banter he experienced with other women. She was a green snake lying in the shadows, unseen but sharp and alive, unpredictable. She was like moving water which sought its own level and meandered to where it needed to be against no obstacle. He could sense that she was less calm on the inside and yet she exuded a languidness while somehow managing to make things happen. He knew he had only seen the smallest tip of her expertise, if he could call it that. He also knew it was not contrived but came naturally to her and unknowingly. As he drove closer to the headquarters and closer to answers, he feared that this woman could be dangerous.

29

It wasn't far he'd told her. From the map, she guessed it was about 20 miles as the crow flies. Not being a crow, it was probably 30 miles. Eve was used to working for hours in the heat and sun, bending over, clipping, planting, dividing bulbs and pulling out murderous couch grass in the gardens of her clients. But she had not trained in the art of long distance hiking in heavy boots and unstable ground, and wasn't sure if she could sustain the momentum for long. It was time for the army boots, of that she was sure. They were still in the jeep with the equipment near. The jeep was to be parked in a secret enclave covered by vines to be picked up later by the village's security forces. They had to rely on their navigation skills and strength.

The jungle rose up to meet her eye as if a living entity, teasing and testing her reliance on her meagre frame. She looked at her hands that most often gave her away. The sweating and shaking was hard to hide and people would comment on it. Strangely enough, her attacks of the mind often went unnoticed to others while it seemed to her that her mind would randomly dissect itself, her eyes unfocused and focused at once, giving her a pounding headache, an anxiousness that took hours to overcome. On these occasions, she was able to withdraw into her plants and have the garden swallow her whole for the length of the episode. Usually there was no one around, no cause and no cure. The pills helped. She'd run out long ago on this involuntary trip and worried how she would cope without the white saviors.

She was surprised that she had survived on little medication. She had never tried cutting back on her intake and was afraid of creating the anxiety the pills were there to ease. The next few days and weeks could be difficult.

The child she had been had managed well enough. Her early school days were not fraught with too much pain. She had buried herself in books to avoid facing people. In later life she had swapped books for plants. Plants were so much more responsive. Every group meeting, classroom discussion, and show and tell had been prepared while suffering days of sweating and anxiety about the event. Presentations in front of the class were common and would start innocuously enough but develop into a head spin and dizziness that enveloped her and seemed to increase her worry and embarrassment. Most times at the beginning she would feign illness knowing she would faint if forced to continue. Later on she just didn't show up. She was an excellent student so the teachers did not mind and she passed her courses with distinctions in spite of the difficulties.

There would, however, always be a comment on her report from the history or French teacher revealing her to be a retiring child in need of special personal development. Her father, though disinterested and unquestioning about most aspects of her life, wanted to see her report and meticulously studied its contents. It was not from fear of him that she doctored her reports before showing him, but merely for the personal embarrassment and further anxiety his knowing would incur. He remained unaware of any condition she had. She had no name for it, only the experience of it taking over her life.

She was gifted, everyone said so. She didn't agree. It was a struggle — not something that came naturally as it did for some people. She knew she had to find a career least exposed to people and performing but one that would allow development of her talents and creativity. She knew she would continue with her studies after school. Perhaps an academic career would suit her but definitely not a teacher. She would pursue the area of least contact with the world, the world of botanical research.

She had started this journey in the belief that she would discover something about her father that she could hold and keep in her heart. Something that would make him more real, have a past that could be shared, even though he could not share it with her. The sudden prospect of meeting the current leader of the party had scared her and she found herself out of her depth, physically and emotionally. She hoped she would be able to continue and not faint in front of the great man. Perhaps he could help her. Once he knew she was in the country, he had asked for her. It was his idea so she had to go along with it. At the moment, she had no choice. The diary told her a little more about her father, and the pictures she had never seen before. It seemed to Eve that the writer had written the poems in a kind of code — a language that would not reveal all to an unknown reader. The words were in English and made sense — and yet they were incomprehensible. There must be a key to the information contained and she hoped San Wu could help. Even though he had requested the meeting, she had been told he was not a man of speed. She may have to wait days or even weeks for him to be in an appropriate mood for an audience.

She reached into her shirt pocket and pulled out the remaining three pills. She had been saving them. Instead of the normal four per day she had been taking only one which had got her this far. The signs of withdrawal had been minimal. She had noticed only a few times of near panic and sweaty palms. She wondered how long that would last when the pills ran out. She had experienced it only once before. The dizziness, heart stopping panic and the blackout, a state of unconsciousness she was told later lasted an hour. She was lucky that time to have people around, people who cared whether she lived or died. She wasn't sure what the response would be surrounded by strangers.

Eve had last worn dusty hiking boots and explorer socks on a research trip to the Kimberley in the north of Western Australia. The rugged red landscape was held together by jagged cliffs and copses of green among the freshwater lakes. Her boots had borne the brunt of these sharp grasping rock faces and she had experienced the relentless heat and dust of the real Australian outback. But there was always a support vehicle waiting with refreshments.

Her boots now had to seek out higher patches of land where no mud puddles had formed from the recent ephemeral downpour of rain. Ever present but not irritating, the rain kept its persistent patter just enough to soak the outer layer of clothing but stopped before it reached the skin. Just as Eve was ready to complain about the dryness and heat, it would rain again.

Josefo, still dressed in army boots and camouflage pants with flak jacket, strode ahead, turning around once in a while to check that she hadn't fallen in a puddle or been kidnapped by a local marauding tribe — both of which were likely scenarios.

'Josefo — how much longer?' She couldn't tell how long they had been walking but it can't have been far.

'Not too far — just over the next hill!' She had heard about 'the next hill' technique before. Just one more and then one more after that. If she'd known how many hills there were to start with she would have collapsed long ago. She felt her legs and feet gain momentum as they forged first one hill then the other. The automatic motion obliterated the thought of pain and just kept the mechanical limbs moving toward their destination.

This man in front of her looked like a city boy, she thought. He seemed sophisticated and knowledgeable about many subjects and yet was equally at home in the jungle, thrashing through the undergrowth, creating a path for her to follow. If he had been brought up in the jungle, he must have spent time in the city and become familiar with many different types of people.

They had switched to light day-packs as Josefo had said it was now only a day's walk. The pack's weight was increasing and Eve felt the strength draining from her.

'Can we stop — I need a rest and some water.'

'Drink as we walk. We can rest at the river's edge. We will be in sight of the village then.'

She kept walking and negotiated the task of drinking while moving. As they reached the top, the gradient flattened out. They moved to the summit together as the path widened out to meet the sky. Their eyes tipped over the ridge to witness the unfolding of a magnificent mountain range suckling against a small but fast-flowing river which was making its rapid route downwards inside the valley. It was a long walk down but the village was just over the river and behind the valley, Josefo said.

She collapsed on a rock near her feet, removed her boots, ripped off her sweaty socks and gave her toes a massage and some air. She opened her water bottle and took a swig. After a moment of relief for toes and thirst, she looked up to see Josefo staring out over the cliff to the valley below.

'It's an amazing country you've got here. It's just a shame the people don't appreciate it.' Eve's passing observation received an angry look from Josefo.

'And do you appreciate your own glorious beaches, mountains and deserts? And what of the indigenous people — do they have equal rights?' Josefo gave her a stare. He had heard about the treatment of native Australians and jumped at the opportunity of pointing out some inadequacies in places other than his own country.

'I'm not saying everything's perfect in Australia. I'm merely commenting on your own land and people — there's no need to get testy about it. It's not personal.'

'Ah but it is.' Josefo turned away and peered over the side of the ledge that had a steep drop below.

'I take my country personally and very seriously. As you should yours. Your country is your identity, even if you do not acknowledge it. It is a powerful force.'

Eve wasn't in the mood for a political discussion she knew she couldn't win. She watched him standing there on the edge of his universe and felt very much alone. He was unpredictable and exciting. She tried to visualize Roger in camouflage pants and an ammo belt and chuckled at the thought. He was best suited to his grey Armani, consulting at his desk. Strictly five star. She thought about the baby he helped conceive and briefly wondered what it was like to have a tiny person growing and developing inside. She had heard from friends about the pain that is then forgotten the first time they hold the tiny infant in their arms. She would never know the feeling.

Her feet were about as good as they were going to get so she gingerly put her boots back on, took another swig of water and stood up.

'Lead on MacDuff!' Josefo looked at her. 'It's an old expression of my father's — nothing personal.'

Josefo re-adjusted his belt and backpack and pointed to a narrow path that seemed to wind its way down the mountains.

'Follow me MacDuff,' he said as he turned towards her with a smile. It was the first time he'd smiled in two days. She realized that he probably had very little trouble getting a date in the mountains, if that's what they called them here. And if such events occurred. There must be women up here somewhere, she thought. Certainly the people she had seen so far looked too seriously occupied with surviving to be worried about romance or candlelit dinners. A candlelit night reconnaissance, maybe. The romancing, she mused, would be rough in these circumstances.

As she walked down the pathway following Josefo she looked out over the mountains. A patch of low-lying cloud was obscuring the highest tips of the mountain range but the earth below was verdant green with thick jungle at its feet thinning out as the mountain grew higher. The contrast of blue sky against green was startling, only softened by the violet blues the shadows cast in the valley. They were heading for the river which she could see from her vantage point was a persistent and virulent stream of water determined to get to its destination, presumably the sea another few hundred miles to the south.

The walk down was not as bad as Eve had

anticipated. The muscles in her legs had strengthened. She felt like her bones and tendons had had the workout of their lives but she was now benefiting. Her boots were earning their living and supplying her feet with well-needed support in the ankles and toes. The trail was smooth, the loose rocks had been washed off by the rain, the earth surface hardened by the sun. It was easier to walk on than mud and soft ground. Her knees were feeling the pressure as the angle continued downwards at 45 degrees.

'Stop looking at the scenery and watch your feet,' commanded Josefo. 'I know the terrain, you do not.'

'Yes, yes. I'm looking down but I also need to see where I'm going, don't I?!'

'Just be cautious — I do not want to have to get you from down there and drag your body back to camp,' he said pointing to a ravine on the right.

'OK — I get your point. Thanks for being so caring!'

Eve soon found that instead of getting harder, the walk and strain on her knees gradually eased as she fell into a comfortable pace. The walking was slow but steady on even ground or a gentle gradient. The time passed quickly until they came upon the river.

They had seen the bridge from a short distance away. Up close it revealed support struts that had been half eaten by termites, missing planks on the suspension body and rope that had not been renewed since the British had landed.

'This is obviously not the bridge used by the locals.'

'They don't seem to want visitors do they — or at least not ones that are easily deterred!'

'This will have to be our entry point. Step where I step.' Josefo set upon the bridge and walking across.

'But what if it won't take both of us?'

'We will find out.' Josefo said as Eve followed him

across the bridge which swayed in the wind. She decided that not looking down was a better option and tried to fix her eyes on the back of Josefo's head. The walk across seemed to take an eternity. The largest obstacle was having to step over wide gaps in the wooden structure and still keep their solid footing. Eve's heart was pounding but she stayed steady, hanging onto the railings and watching Josefo in front of her. They made it across and looked back at the derelict bridge, unused for years. Turning back to the village, Josefo pointed to his right.

'Look there — the new bridge! I knew there was one.' It had been hidden behind a small mound in the terrain, only meters from the bridge they had just crossed. Eve could see it from where she stood, its shiny metal railings supported by glistening new planks of wood on the main structure.

'I thought you needed a little adventure. You enjoy, yes?'

'That's not fair when I'm exhausted!' He laughed aloud as he urged her forward to the township.

'We will need to go to admin hut first to get allocated lodgings. I will go in.' As they walked past the gates and into the main compound of the township, a small crowd formed around them. The township was spread out over acreage with many huts of varying sizes dotted around in no particular pattern.

Eve didn't know yet, but this small village would be her home for some time.

30

*T*he ghost had awakened after roaming the nights for a long time. It was only now that the child in her could see the vision that had terrified her for as long as she could remember — a slim, tall shape, groundless and hovering and not of this earth, she knew. She had thought it was evil, mocking, terrifying, white. She had always imagined its cold touch, its hidden force waiting to be released. Now it was here — it had come for her. She was no longer frightened — could no longer scream. A gentle breeze moved the curtains aside and she could see it clearly — he wasn't a monster, a creature from her past that had haunted her every memory. He was here. He was real, she was sure. She looked more closely at the space made by the fluttering curtain. She saw his face. Was it the face of evil? But his was not an evil face. The face of a man, that was all. She was afraid and yet she yearned for him.

'Do not be alarmed — I have not come to hurt you,' he began. 'I have come to take you to a better place — somewhere away from here. Somewhere you'll be happy.' He stretched out his hand, she stretched out hers expecting the cold of night but instead met the warmth of his touch.

It was Ko Tan's face she felt, his warmth asleep beside her. Mya opened her eyes now the dream was over again. She hadn't screamed this time — or had she? Sometimes she could not tell. Other times her throat hurt so much she knew that her voice had practiced scaring the demons away. Her heart was beating, her body shed a cold sweat, her hair was dank and wet.

She rolled over to one side and felt the pain inside her, remembered pain that would never go away. The distaste would subside but not the memory, one added to a million more would make no difference. Her eyes opened to the night.

The reconnaissance had not been successful, she remembered. No more elixir and more money paid for no result. How many times had she said this would not happen again? But she was caught — and always by a man, she thought bitterly. She looked at the body lying next to her in his bed. The long limbs, not young, but nimble and agile like a young man who had extracted pleasure from her brownness. The hands that caressed her naked frame every night releasing her tautness and relieving her feelings of despair. She looked at this man who had saved her life more times than she could remember, and was repulsed by him. His skin stretched across bones scarcely beneath the surface, while his big head tottered to one side with the mouth slightly open breathing out its spit to the pillow. His angular feet protruding through the covers of the night made her throat contract and her breath raspy. His pride and joy was lying limp across the top of his thigh, now a thing with no substance that would soon pump joy to its inert status. How she had stroked and cajoled this marshmallow flesh into an organism ready to fight for its territory. It was now dying, almost afraid. Such a vulnerable tortoise with no shell, unprotected against the ravages of rain. How could she restrain herself from its ultimate protection — the god of men, their gold, their being, their lust.

She looked again and saw his body turn exposing a plump pillow of flesh that she had only seen in moonlight. Her hand stretched out to caress this flesh. How she had fallen into those long, smooth arms so many times after the first: willingly, mindlessly, lovingly knowing his fingers could ignite her from within and send her to places she had visited but not dwelled in. She had so longed to be a permanent resident there. Now she knew she was.

Looking at him, she knew she could destroy his love. She had tried but he was still there sleeping beside her, riding that white horse in the night so often she could feel the hardness of the saddle as he pulled her up beside him and they belted back up the hill to the house and to safety.

But she would never feel safe.

31

Four weeks and there was still no word of a meeting with the great San Wu. Josefo had told her stories of how the village had begun, San Wu's passion, the construction of the casino and bowling alley at odds with its mountainous location. She had willed herself to believe that being here waiting to meet him had been a fortuitous event, it was meant to be. She could attain her goal. At least, from what she'd heard about him, he knew the history. Had he known her father? And so she waited.

Eve tried to be patient but was beginning to find the village life less than idyllic. Conditions were basic, most lived in simple huts with little ventilation, no plumbing and a tap for water in a kind of outdoor communal shower. The hut she had was more private and secure although she was aware of the vast numbers of men around her with few women. Most of them had fled with the last evictions. There were no children.

She was aware that Josefo's hut was not far from hers which gave her a strange feeling of comfort. He had begun to talk more and they mostly ate their meals together in a large dining hall also used by the soldiers. They tolerated inquisitive and peering eyes which she chose to ignore but the staring gradually lessened. Not many could speak English so she was spared unnecessary socializing or questioning. She realized how odd it must look to others — this strange foreigner brought to a village against her will, and now taking a meal with the person who had kidnapped her.

She had not spotted San Wu or anyone who looked vaguely like a leader. There was no sign of him and Josefo had relayed to her the message from some soldiers that he had not been seen by anyone — or anyone who was allowed to say — for two years.

Eve began to feel the dark cloud of uncertainty weigh on her consciousness.

Though Josefo had his own hut, he stayed from time to time in the men's quarters, full of rows of single beds. He told her he found the camaraderie of the men pleasing after the trip in the jungle and liked listening to the different dialects they spoke.

Eve had found herself waking early every day and walking to the top of the adjacent hill to watch the sunrise. It was always spectacular and she wallowed in the gloriousness of the colors of the morning skies. Josefo had told her not to venture past this point to any crop yards or further to the border. There were many disparate groups of rebels with one cause or another only too willing to kill on sight. At the top of the hill, she could make out newly cleared land and rows of green leafy low-lying shrubs that she had come to recognize as the poppy plant. They were visible even from this vantage point — rows and rows over an amount of acreage she could not estimate.

She felt ill at the amount of forest that had been felled to produce this catalyst for death and could not stop thinking about Papa Chau Lap's words. She hoped he would be able to make contact with her again. She wondered how many had survived the long walk south.

32

E ve came to know some of the few women who were still in their homes, older wives of men who had stayed to tend their crops and help with the cultivation of the poppy. She had learnt a few basic words of Burmese and could carry on a conversation using facial expressions and hand gestures. She had found some old Burmese books on a shelf in her hut. She couldn't read the text but amused herself with looking at the photographs of villages, the way they had looked for thousands of years. She learnt to meditate. She had tried it at home for a few weeks but her frenetic internal superhighway could not quiet. She grew bored easily and only lasted in her lotus position for a few minutes before squirming as though freeing herself from leg irons. When she realized she had nothing else to do after her morning walk, she sat in the position and practiced the mantra that was taught to her many months before. She found, with no other distractions that it began to work. At first, confusion reigned in her head, thousands of images and voices swam into her mind's vision all fighting for the number one spot. Eventually, they eased and she found that hours would pass quickly.

Eve could not stop herself from wondering about San Wu. She had heard so many rumors. First she saw him as a huge man, with massive arms and enormous head. At other times, she pictured him covered in tattoos with scars all over his face. Or was he a military genius, a brilliant strategist who debated expertly on political subjects?

Late one afternoon, Josefo knocked on her door.

'The time has come. He will see you now.'

'What? Right now? I have to get ready. Prepare myself! Will he let me go then? I don't belong here.'

'Now. Just come. We must walk up the hill to his quarters and the big hall.'

Eve checked her reflection in the mirror, and grabbed a brush to run through her hair after her walk to the hilltop. She put the diary in the pocket of her army pants which had become her uniform. She followed Josefo's lead and started heading up the pathway to the new buildings on the hill.

33

E ve and Josefo were at the entrance to a long room, elegant with dark-colored wood on all walls and below their feet, a hand-made red carpet with hand-stitched silk from the mountains of Burma. The carpet stretched out before them ending in a high chair more like a throne with intricately carved backing, arms and legs. They had been impressed by the Tang dynasty solid oak doors girded by thick steel bands and huge bolts. The building was not old but had been created from some old materials and designed to look ancient from the beginning. And now they waited.

It was to be a few minutes more but more minutes after waiting for weeks would not be a struggle. Eve was anxious, more than she had been for some time. She didn't break out in a sweat or get dizzy. She felt a cacophony in her stomach and needed water. She was no more anxious than most people at a job interview, she thought. She could get through this. She pushed her hand into the pocket of her pants and felt the familiar hard back of the small diary. It crossed her mind that it may not be appropriate for a woman to meet the great leader San Wu wearing camouflage pants but there was little she could do about it.

They were given silk cushions on which to kneel

while the wait continued. Most of the locals sat this way or in the crouching position which they found comfortable. The cushion turned out to be an adequate resting place for her crossed legs and, much to her surprise, she managed to sustain the position indefinitely.

She looked over at Josefo who had his head lowered and his hands in his lap in reverence to the throne, she guessed. Eve hadn't picked him for a conformist — there was more to learn about him. As she waited, Eve noticed the absence of sun in this late afternoon. There were large windows she had seen from outside the building but they were now covered by heavy curtains colored red to match the carpet. The only light emanated from one huge candle sitting on a dais next to the throne surrounded by many smaller candles all glowing alive in the half light.

There was a slight rustling sound from the front of the room near the dais and two men walked to each side of the throne. Eve noticed they were not large men, just average sized Burmese though with large upper arms and well-developed chests. They could have been body builders, Eve thought. They were dressed in the usual military fatigues but there was something different about their attire. They were excessively clean, their boots shone and their uniforms had sparkling new lanyards and epaulettes. Their caps were pristine. They reeked elite. As she saw the soldiers take their place next to the throne, Eve started rising to her feet. She anticipated that the next entrant would be San Wu and her turn to meet him. She was nervous but able to contain herself and now felt the thrill of excitement as a prelude to an audience.

Just as she was rising, one of the soldiers put out his arm to stop her.

'It is not time. Be patient,' said the soldier.

Josefo turned to Eve and whispered close to her ear. 'I have heard he likes to play games. We have to wait, Eve.' This was one of the rare moments he called her Eve. It sounded strange. She was learning patience now — a skill she had not mastered in her own country.

They waited three hours for the great man to make an appearance. Boredom and inertia had taken their toll on Eve. Her legs were sore and her body weary from the wait. She had long since given up any pretense of anticipation so when San Wu did show himself, she was hardly aware of him. Josefo had to knock her arm to re-energize her for the meeting to come.

At his insistence, she looked up and saw a very unusual sight. Imaginings and reality were often disparate creatures but the reality and fantasy of this man were on two far different scales.

As Eve took in the apparition before her, she began to feel uneasy about her position in the village and her future. There was something about this man, even from a distance that made her heart go cold. She could see the figure move from behind the curtains and place himself on the throne that had been waiting as long as Eve for his presence.

Josefo and Eve were motioned by the waiting soldiers to move forward and position themselves in front of the great man. They rose to their feet, aching joints and muscles creaking in rebellion. Once on their feet, they walked side by side down a red carpet. Eve wondered what had been the fate of others walking this journey.

Eve moved her hand to Josefo's, touching his little finger. It twitched and closed around her thumb. Linked, they moved forward until they reached the throne where they were again motioned by the soldiers

— this time to stop. Two small stools were whisked behind their legs and the weary Eve felt her legs thank her. They found themselves close to San Wu now but not at his level. They were far below him at ground level.

Eve looked up to view the countenance of the man she had been waiting to meet for so long. She could tell he was a small man even as he sat on his bejeweled chair. His head was slightly too large for his body and his face had a sallow complexion. He was not black or white — but somewhere in a no man's land of ash.

He was wearing the uniform of camouflage pants and shirt but with new epaulettes like his soldiers. Unlike his soldiers, he had a chest that glittered with medals of all sizes. The weight of the medals must have tilted him forward slightly as he appeared to be bending at an odd angle. He had across his body the ubiquitous ammunition sling. A black beret sat neatly perched on his head. His hands were gloved. This seemed rather odd to Eve until her eyes dropped to his feet where she beheld a pair of the most exquisite, pink Chinese slippers.

She looked from the slippers to Josefo's blank face and up to the man on the throne. She studied his face as if to dive into his subconscious and read his thoughts. She saw nothing and began to wonder how this man who aspired to be a leader for so long had turned into something far different. Without him uttering a single word and in the space of roughly five minutes she realized she could be at risk. But she wanted to talk, to discover for herself what this man was like and what he knew about her father.

*

San Wu had entered the room at a leisurely pace interested to see what this foreigner held for him. He no longer held audiences, that privilege had ended when he had let go of the last troops in the mountains. He had in the past loved this ritual of subservience to a greater power and had believed he held the secret to the future of the world. Since the helicopters and US satellites had invaded his territory he was not so sure. There was still a need for the theatre and he was always happy to entertain overseas visitors. They had an image of him that was shattered by the end of the meeting. San Wu was not considered to be predictable nor did he want to be. He would remain an enigma for as long as possible and never do what the foreigners expected of him.

He had prepared himself well as usual. A game of ten pin bowls before breakfast, a meeting with his congress and a nap before taking the throne. He carefully chose his dress and shaved leaving a slight vertical line of hair on his chin, fashionable even in the hills. His steps were measured as he drew back the curtain and took his place on the velvet-covered throne where he had held court with often deadly outcomes for the participants. Apart from foreign journalists, many did not manage to leave the village alive. As he took his seat he was soothed by the Chinese slippers tight against the sides of his feet. He looked down to admire his slippers.

His eyes connected with Eve's as she raised her head to look.

For the first time, he acknowledged them both with a slight nod of his head. San Wu was still sitting when he decided to speak.

'How good of you to come,' he began in thickly accented English. 'My name is San Wu — welcome to Hilltop Ravine. It is an unusual name for a village, is it not and not very well named. Neither on a hill nor in a ravine, the village sits in between these two landforms like a child between its parents, sheltering from the storm. I trust you have comfortable quarters?' He stopped and looked from one to the other with a blank expression. Eve was loath to answer what she thought was a redundant question as he would have known the conditions of each hut, and surely the circumstances of her entry.

Eve bowed her head and closed her eyes to let Josefo take up the retort.

'It is a pleasure to see you after so long, Sir — we have missed you visiting the ranks. We are completely comfortable. Thank you for asking, Sir!'

'Mmmm — and what is your position in my army, young man? Remind me?'

'I have been anointed as soon-to-be second in charge, Sir. A position I will humbly accept with the utmost gratitude.'

'Yes, yes I remember. And this must be the Australian woman, Eve Robinson, is it not?' San Wu raised himself from his velvet pouch and walked close to the edge of the dais closely surveying Eve. He pronounced her surname 'Lobinson'.

Josefo volunteered that it was indeed the Australian and they had spent days travelling in the jungle to get here and had spent weeks in the camp.

'Very good — you have experienced some of the exquisite yet challenging jungle and the varied species it holds, did you not?' Eve felt she had to answer.

'I've been brought here against my will and demand to be released!' she sounded more confident than she felt.

'Indeed!' San Wu threw back.

'And I met some locals who are very unhappy at their treatment under your regime.' Josefo kicked her foot.

'Unhappy — who? None I have met in many years are unhappy — they must be Indian or Thai?'

'They were your own people. A farmer and his clan had been ousted from their village and made to walk 300 miles to a new settlement. Do you think this is just?'

She was in waist high now and more calm as each minute passed.

'Just? Yes — what might you think is the meaning of this word — its real meaning — in your own country? Do you have a justice system you admire?'

Eve was tired of another reference to her own country and she didn't want to get into a political or cultural discussion about Australia's policies. It was a clever technique.

'The justice system to speak of is here — San Wu, if I may call you that. Your people are being unwillingly relocated and under your leadership.'

'Firstly, you need to understand this country and its people before you can make judgments about its laws. Far from being forcibly moved, these people have been offered land — fertile and free land — and a livelihood far greater than they would ever have had in the mountains. The land by the sea has much more fertile soil capable of producing ten times the redeemable crop for market. They are far better off no matter how they present that to a foreigner.'

Eve had been told that the soil closer to the sea was laterite and well leached of most nutrients needed to grow rice crops — the predominant crop grown after highland poppies.

'They are unhappy about walking for three months, having members of their family die on the road and then reaching their destination only to find disease and poor soil unfit for growth!' She focused her stare directly at him and felt her throbbing head beginning to overtake her senses.

He didn't speak for a moment and then said: 'How do you like my footwear — very fashionable, is it not?'

Eve turned to Josefo whose eyes were now aimed at the pink glow of the sequined Chinese slippers before looking down to see San Wu's feet dangling from the velvet throne.

'Ah — yes,' Eve managed. Just as she was about to offer him a bridge to her next issue, he blurted, 'Now I am ready to see your diary.'

'But — how did you know about that?'

'I have a thousand eyes and ears, Ms Lobinson — never forget that. Come upon the dais.'

Eve walked to the side of the dais and was helped up by San Wu's bodyguards. She was offered a large cushion covered in silk fabric. She found a comfortable position and crossed her legs.

San Wu placed himself opposite her on a similar cushion — as pink as his slippers.

'Let us see this document and discover what it is you want to know. I know how you came by it but who is the author?'

'The people I am ... was staying with believed it to be someone called Alexandra,' said Eve.

'Ah yes, your grandmother, wife of the Tiger, your grandfather, Raoul!'

'They didn't tell me that!' Eve paused. 'They just told me she had died recently.' She looked at San Wu to see his reaction.

'Alexandra dead! I see ... yes that would be so.' He closed his eyes.

'But I need to know more about what it means — I don't understand what it's saying.'

Eve pulled the diary from the shin pocket of her

camouflage pants and handed it to San Wu.

'Firstly, Eve — may I call you Eve? What is it that you do in your country?' San Wu moved closer to her.

'I am a horticulturalist — plants are my passion — you know, the varied species of flora — the intermixings — how they grow, where and with which other plants. I have an affinity with and love of the environment.' Eve found the conversation going her way.

'But your country is a desert, is it not? What can you possibly grow there?'

'Oh — a lot of it is desert, but the peripheral coastal regions and some inland territory is rich land able to sustain many species — it is varied in flowering plants and natives.'

San Wu sat back on his cushion, closed his eyes and did not speak. Eve looked down at Josefo who was still on his cushion in front of the throne but still able to hear the conversation. He gave Eve an encouraging nod and when she looked back at San Wu, he had opened his eyes and was reading the diary. He read the few pages that were given to him while his expression remained unchanged. He laid the book onto his cushion and placed his hands on his crossed knees.

'What do you know of the Tiger?' he asked.

'I haven't heard of him ... you say he was my grandfather?' Eve was taken aback by his sudden change in manner but was willing to play the game.

'Raoul, Alexandra you have heard of now — and Poi Trang — have you heard this name before?'

'No.'

'What do you know of the beginnings of the Freedom Party and its history — are you aware of its founding members?'

'Ah no — I don't know.'

San Wu's stare was grave and he spat out a word

she didn't understand.

'You know nothing — what have you to reveal to me? Nothing!'

'You forced me here!' she spat back.

He muttered a few words of his native language, rose from the pillow and strode to the other side of the dais. He sighed, walked back to his cushion, sat down and stretched.

'What do you want from me, foreign woman? Why have you come here? Do you intend some trickery or are you just stupid?'

Josefo stood and started striding toward the dais. The two bodyguards barricaded him from the area around San Wu.

'You come here through the jungle, call my people unhappy and demand help from me. Why should I help you and not kill you now as a nuisance to our cause?' Eve was surprised at his sudden change in mood.

'I was kidnapped and brought here!' said Eve. She stopped herself. 'But I have information you need.' She realized this man was in control of her life as no other man had ever been.

'Yes, go on ...'

She paused.

'I know how to propagate the poppy plant to create one plant ten times its size — your revenues will increase exponentially!'

'And what know you of the Burmese poppy plant — you a foreigner who has been here five minutes?'

'It is my job to study and understand the horticultural species of every country in the world so that I know each condition for growing the best crops. I have been studying crop genetics for years and now have an idea about not only harvesting the plant but harvesting revenue. I began to think of this idea when my father died and I learned of the Burma connection. I just need a mentor to help me create the environment for its optimum growth. Unless you can let me go ...?'

Josefo looked stunned. There were two possibilities. Eve had made the whole thing up or she had deceived him from the beginning. Either way, she was in dangerous waters. San Wu was intrigued.

'Alex is dead ... I am sorry about that,' he said. Eve's face softened.

'You knew him ...'.

'Of course. What makes you think that I have anything to do with rearing this poppy that produces the cream that kills? We are harvesting legitimate tobacco in these hills. Do you know the difference?'

She recalled her third year assignment at university on the cultivation of Sri Lankan tobacco fields cultivation and struggled to remember some salient facts that would support her argument. But he knew her father.

'I'm sure you are not knowingly growing this evil plant but I do know that it is being grown in these hills. As a horticulturist my aim is to produce a cultivated plant with no expectation of outcome — even though I know what that outcome will be. *Papaver somniferum* can produce many types of product including morphine and heroin. I can also cultivate D-Lysergic Acid Amide, mescaline and smokable DMT. Tell me about my father.'

If he believed she could do it, he would protect her and she could trade information. It was risky with more than a small chance of failure but her options were running out. She was not sure she could count on Josefo, whom she knew was tipped to be 2IC.

'You will help me, as I will help you. Do you have a choice?'

As San Wu closed his eyes and looked to the

ceiling, she took it as an opportunity to provide him no answer. She glanced at Josefo and then looked back to the small man propped up on the cushion in front of her.

'What do you want to know?' he said.

'I need to know about my father's past, what happened to him, why the diary is important and what it reveals. I want to know my father. And my mother.'

'I fear that is too late — he is dead.'

'Yes — he passed away just before I came to Burma...'

He paused. 'You are naïve if you are not aware of my network. I know everything — even before you think it,' San Wu smiled.

'I suppose I am. I would like to know my father other than as the man in the grey cardigan.'

'If I tell you the past of what I know, you will stay here for three months or until you produce this so-called hyperplant you speak of — whichever comes first. Then you can go.' And never leave, he would have added but he had learned from previous meetings with foreigners that they responded better to surprises rather than knowing their fate from the start. He thought this young woman could be of help to him. She might have knowledge he could leverage with the country's leader, Poi Trang.

*

Eve understood the deal. Stay and get the information in exchange for this revenue-generating hyperplant or get no information and leave now — if indeed she could. She had come this far, she was prepared to take the risk.

As she looked at San Wu she imagined she saw her father standing next to him. He was very different from how she remembered him. Like an old photo, he had was surrounded by edges of sepia. He was a young man, vibrant, alive. Though there were no colors, he was the essence of a color he had lost in later life. His clothes were different, something of the past, of a different culture and of strength. He was not happy or sad but was holding his hand out to Eve gesturing her to come to him. She blinked and the image vanished. She stretched out her hand to touch his but in its disintegration she was left reaching.

'I do not tolerate interruptions so listen well.' San Wu placed himself on the velvet throne, put his hands on the carved arms and readjusted his ammunition belt. He crossed one leg over the other and began to caress his pink slipper. He started to speak.

34

'I was a young man when I first met your grandfather, the Tiger, and not much older when your father entered the scene. Your father and I were never friends. I did not think he was a leader and I did not think he should be groomed for it just because he was Raoul's son. I never allowed myself to get to know him in those early years. Most of the time I was training in the mountains, so the stories I did not witness myself have been told to me by other members who were present at the time.'

I came to know Raoul very well. In fact, he became a father figure to me. My own father had stayed in my village when I left at an early age and I never saw him again. He had never been a father to me in what I consider to be the proper sense of the word. It was my mother who brought me up. My father was away and left my mother alone for long periods of time. As I would. I was in need of a father's attention when I joined a local band of fighters. One night on a reconnaissance, we came across a group of about 20 men on a hillside farm. We were thirty strong and believed we could outfight this band of old men. We were wrong. They had us surrounded and defeated within half an hour. Most of us were only children. I was sixteen with no experience of battle. We joined the group at their insistence and I met Raoul, the man who would be my mentor and father. I found him to be strong and warm. I worshipped him and tried to model myself on him. I liked him, yes, I must admit I did in those early years. He told me some of his experiences — I may well be the only one he told — other than his wife. Alexandra, writer in this book you have.

He came to this country as a white man. He left it as an inhabitant of a country he loved and vowed to protect. He told me of his desires to create a balance in our country, of peace and freedom but above all of humanity to all beings.

He told me how he had gathered a few of his trusted friends and colleagues, about ten like-minded men. Once a week they would meet at his home. The discussions began quietly with Raoul taking notes of all decisions. I remember him telling me about these days with great fondness. In the beginning, they were all passionate and he believed that he could be the turning point in the fight for freedom. But one member of the group remained quiet throughout the proceedings for several months while the talk became stronger. This man spoke of revolution which Raoul opposed. The man became aggressive until Raoul threw him out of the group. Late the next week while they were having their weekly gathering, the military police arrived to escort Raoul to the barracks. He had no choice but to go with them. Raoul was arrested for conspiring against the government and he was left in a cell awaiting trial for three years. The trial did not happen and no charges could be laid for any offence. He was released.

A different man emerged from prison. He said he felt different too. Because of experiencing the injustice of prison for three years with no trial, he realized a new force was required. From a strong, warm and confident fighter emerged a bitter, angry and determined man. The betrayal by his former friend and colleague had weighed on him heavily for those three years and he had planned a strategy to put in place on his release. He said he was overjoyed to see his 10-year-old son and was even more determined to protect him from the ravages of this corrupt government.

Undeterred by his imprisonment, and in fact inspired, he started the gatherings again which he named the Freedom Party. One thing changed. He now acted under the cover of darkness, in secret. He found a deserted shack far up in the mountains at the back of his property. That shack became the new meeting place. Instead of disintegrating, the group had more followers and by the end of three months, 75 men were regularly meeting in this jungle headquarters.

As time went on, Raoul's reputation as a leader of freedom grew. The 75 men were from respected professions and at a high level in many industries. Through their influence and powers of persuasion, many injustices were stopped, journalists were set free. They also started a newspaper to encourage communication, not propaganda, just reporting on decisions the government was making. After a while, Raoul was more angry at the system. He decided this group needed more than just meetings, passing resolutions, and providing a means of communication. The ethnic groups had been allowed the vote and there had been fewer incidents of no-trial judgments. Soon this changed. The military junta staged a coup, overtook the already corrupt government and now, in his opinion, criminals were in power. People from different ethnic groups were going missing, people arrested if they couldn't show birth certificates, journalists imprisoned again.

Raoul knew action was needed. He started night reconnaissance, kidnapping and torture of the opposing force to gain intelligence about the ruling junta's movements that took him to the edge of the law. His reputation had spread. Among the freedom party he was known as the Tiger. He could never let his real name be known. He had a small group of five trusted friends who knew each other's true identity.

Raoul decided that his son Alex, now 15, should become a part of the growing Freedom movement.

Raoul needed Alex home to attend the weekly meetings in the mountains and to start learning about the cause. He would also need to be taught the skills that would keep him alive and protect his team. It would not be easy for the boy — he had had it soft for a long time. That time was over.

Raoul told me the first year was hard for Alex but he managed to learn what was required of him and survive life in the jungle. The relationship between father and son developed and a deep respect grew between them. Raoul was pleased with his progress.

It was around this time that I met Alex for the first time. I was 21 and had learned much from Raoul about military strategy and strength. He entrusted me with the job of teaching Alex everything he had taught me. I was not happy. This boy had taken my role as the son. I knew I was not Raoul's son but we had developed such a close relationship that when Alex arrived, I was angry that I had been pushed aside just because this was his own flesh and blood. But it was what Raoul wanted. Alex was a good student, I could not deny that. Raoul had promised me the leadership once he had gone — he often said he would only leave if he was forced by death — I believed him. He had trained me in this role for five years and then Alex came and I knew that the leadership would no longer be mine. I began to hate this boy.'

*

San Wu stood up then knelt down close to Eve.

'As you can see, this is not the end of the story. Knowledge is a valuable commodity and now you must give me something of yours. Your diary, please.'

Eve did not want to let it leave her hands and struggled to find something to say.

'But it was the last thing I found in my father's dying hands. I can't let it go! Please have some respect for my heritage!' She didn't know if San Wu respected anything but she was prepared to try.

'I can take it from you forcefully but I choose not to. I will speak to you again and I will get the diary from you willingly next time.'

'I will give you one more thing,' He looked at her gravely. 'You still have blood relatives alive.'

Eve looked up suddenly weary. Her face asked for the answer.

'You will have to wait for next time. Be sure to bring the diary. Remember do not stray too far from camp. And I want to see some results from you in a week. Go.'

35

Mya tried to remember her parents. Hardworking parents certainly, but loving, weren't they? Long days followed very long nights which merged to make up her life. What had it been? It was short, yes. She'd had a family once but no more — not blood relatives anyway. Not after they'd taken her. She struggled to remember the people, the faces, anything. It was no longer easy. The faces were fading and the memories intermittent. Whenever she thought back, her heart raced and her temples pulsed — she was hot and wouldn't cool down for hours. It hurt to try to remember. Her body still felt the pain and her heart tried to remember a time when it didn't ache. Her mother had loved her, hadn't she? Why then did she flinch every time she saw the exchange of money, vendors in the street, mothers and babies, traders on vegetable wagons. She pushed her mind to look into long-hidden corners but she could make nothing of it. Ko Tan had told her not to worry, to forget, to think only about now and how secure she was. But she couldn't forget and yet she couldn't remember. Small dark places terrified her.

Flashes of memory would come to her. Flashes of working with her mother sometimes picking fruit, other times preparing the berries and corn that would make their evening meal. Her father was gone for most of the day only returning at dusk, dirty and hungry. Yet he always had a hug and a kind word for her in those very young years. She had several pets that she grew to love as her own children, children that she often dreamed of having before she was very old. She had three dogs, lovable old mongrels who showed their loyalty to her day after day awaiting her every instruction. Schooling was infrequent at best but some classes were held with the other children on the farm in a makeshift shack with a rotating roster of parents who could spare a couple of hours in the day.

One memory was too painful to bring to the surface. His memory. Why could she picture his face so clearly and yet remember nothing of her early years with him? She struggled to remember any details about their early lives. There was only one detail she remembered. This one was pain, this one she longed to forget. But she never forgot his face. She touched the pendant she wore around her neck. It was antique silver, the only thing of value she had been able to keep, and only through deception and subterfuge. She had been lucky to keep it through her rough, tumbling journey over her short life. It was worn from her caress. She clasped it now pulling it away from her pumping heart, the warmth of her skin mellowing the still shining metal in her fingers. She caressed it between her fingers as she had done countless times. The rubbing always conjured images of people from the past, her family, their faces slowly diminished by time. She remembered herself at 10, laughing and looking up from the crop she had just planted, one of her beloved dogs in the background looking expectantly, smiling its dog grin, eyes closed in warmth. She knew her laugh was there, her teeth white and exposed, her eyes bright with the expectation of a life unlived, and of tears unshed. And then, she remembered the face of her beloved brother, older, the most beautiful person she had known, her protector, her savior and her blood. Her Josefo.

Her throat constricted and she fought the well-known urge to cry. She would never again cry for him.

36

Josefo closed the door to the approaching storm. It was August when the storm season was at its peak. The days disappeared into a watery mist by afternoon and by night, continuous rain. He knew the seasons well and had not minded the rain. It gave relief and softened the landscape, smoothed out the edges that were hard to erode. The land was used to it too. The plants had developed strong sinuous root systems to hang on to mother soil while the rains tried to tear them away from the breast of the earth.

It had been a long day for them both but he wondered how Eve was holding up after the interview with the great man. He was worried that she had immersed herself in hot water with that story of creating some super plant. What was she thinking? He was sure she was lying. She couldn't have kept that to herself all this time and then just changed the direction on him like that, could she? He pushed the thought to the back of his head but thinking about Eve as not so innocent interested him. He figured she was intelligent even though she came across as a bit uptight and vague. She had certainly turned herself around on the last stretch.

He remembered them both leaving the auditorium with San Wu still on his throne. Just as they were near the great oak door, San Wu raised his arm and a guard stopped Josefo in his tracks.

'Come.' The guard pointed to the great man as he escorted Eve further out into the night. Josefo walked again along that red carpet where they had waited for so long earlier in the day. As he reached San Wu, the older man put out his hand and touched Josefo's shoulder.

'Do one thing for me and you will prove your loyalty — and an unrivalled and sure place as second-in-charge. You will then be ready to take over from me — it will not be long.' San Wu gave a rasping cough and looked at Josefo.

'Get me her diary — and get it tonight. That diary belongs to me — it is rightfully mine! Any way you can. Now go. Come back tomorrow. You will not have to wait very long.' San Wu rose from his velvet throne and disappeared behind the curtain.

So this was his mission. He had chosen to accept it without saying a word. Had that been agreement? He wasn't sure himself but as San Wu believed he would do it, what else could he now do but carry out the great man's wishes.

As he left the long room, he had a strange feeling in his heart. Something familiar, unpleasant, remembered from the past. He pushed it to the side as he had often done, not acknowledging or willing to bring it to the front of his consciousness. It remained deep within him, a hard nob of charcoal he could not budge. He would sleep with it again that night, and wake up with it the next morning, and the next.

The rain had begun and he had to run to his hut to avoid getting soaked. Not that he minded — he was used to this weather and was grateful that he had at least comfortable quarters and not just a tree or tent to shelter in for the night which was his usual abode. He felt it was late. There was no one walking around the village and the men's quarters only had one or two lights left on so it must have been past 10 o'clock.

He looked over at Eve's hut. Her light was on but it was dim, she must have only a lamp on in the room. Perhaps she was reading. Maybe she was rereading the parts of the diary she didn't understand, trying to think about her father and the life he must have had. Or she could be having a drink although he had never seen her drink and didn't think she seemed the type to be drinking on her own at night. She could be meditating as Josefo himself sometimes did. As a Buddhist he had developed some mastery in this art even though he hadn't practiced it for a long time. At one time in his life it had given him much peace. He wished he made time for it now — but there was no time. And he didn't deserve to be calm and at peace any more. He could tolerate suffering. Yet meditating didn't seem like Eve's thing either. Perhaps she was writing in her own journal. He remembered she had asked for pen and paper from one of the militia and they had seen no harm in it. She was certainly diligent and was probably already planning her crop rotation or whatever it was she had to plan to make San Wu believe her story. If it was a story. Anyway, she was up and probably not averse to a late night visitor. This could be his chance. He had to strike soon or the fear and anger would take over and he would never be able to obey the command, or have the opportunity to lead.

In his cabin, he rifled through the top drawer of the cabinet beside his bed and found a bottle of whiskey. He put it in the inside pocket of his jacket, left the room and closed the door behind him.

He jogged over to the small verandah outside her hut to avoid the beginnings of a wet night. As he stepped onto the wooden boards, he shook his head and dusted off some light rain that had landed on his clothes and hair. He tried to look into the open window, but Eve had closed the curtains and he could see nothing from where he stood, just the dim glow of a light from within.

He stood facing the door and was about to knock when he noticed his hand was shaking. He forced it to meet the door, the sound loud in the silence. He waited for a few moments thinking he would hear movement in the room as Eve got up to answer the door. He heard nothing. Just as he raised his hand to knock again, Eve swung open the door and he almost hit her in the face with his fist. He held back as she recoiled slightly and appeared to be unsteady on her feet, her eyes red and puffed. She was wearing a white singlet top and shorts.

'Whoa — I'm getting there!' she said.

'I thought you might be asleep. Are you OK?' She didn't look like the Eve he knew. He had never seen her out of control.

'So you thought you'd wake me up. Nice. Well now you're here and I'm obviously not asleep, you may as well come in out of the rain.'

Eve opened the door wider and he entered the small space of her hut.

'Welcome to my Taj Mahal, please make yourself comfortable, Mr potential number 2.' He had just sat down in the only chair in the room, and looked up at her as she placed herself on the edge of the bed, the only space left to sit on.

'What do you mean?'

'Why didn't you tell me you had ambitions to be the great leader? I shared my stuff! I didn't take you for a liar.'

'I did not come here for insults and I did not hide anything from you. You did not ask me what my ambitions were.'

'So now I'm interested.'

'Yes and I am interested in how you are going to develop some super plant for San Wu. Seems like you have been lying to me.'

'I had to think of something to keep myself here. Otherwise he would find out I have no information for him. I'm not stupid. I can tell I'm on thin ice — or slippery mud might be a better analogy in this part of the world.'

She looked down and he saw something had dropped on the floor. He bent over and picked up a small photo in a simple frame. It was a man, fair complexioned with hair to match, wearing a suit sitting in front of a desk. He looked vaguely familiar.

'My father,' said Eve with a sadness Josefo had not seen in her before. 'He's coming alive to me here.'

'What is wrong — you look sad. Is it about your father?' Josefo had not practiced this sort of empathy very much but he knew what he was expected to say.

'I have been thinking about him a lot.' He noticed her eyes were red, watery and puffy with dark rings underneath. She reminded him of a night creature he had disturbed from its nest once, its eyes like a newborn unseeing and vulnerable.

Josefo reached into his jacket pocket and pulled out the bottle. Scotch.

'Some?' He offered her the bottle.

'I'll get a glass — two even.' She moved over to a cupboard and pulled out two spirit glasses. He poured two fingers in each.

'Sorry — no ice. How primitive.' She sipped at the glass like a chipmunk on a large nut, nibbling and sucking at the liquid cautiously at first, then taking more with each mouthful. Josefo downed the drink in one and had another poured before she had taken a second sip.

'You're better at this than me,' said the chipmunk.

He had eased into the chair and with his third drink nicely warm in his throat, he felt as if he could stay all night. It was a possibility, and he thought about it. He hadn't considered it before. He was just going to get her drunk and take the diary. She would know fairly soon after that but by then he wouldn't care. Now he had another plan. If he could get her into bed, she might not notice it was missing for a while, or at the very least, feel too awful to accuse him. He would have her by then, his charms would have worked. He could give it a try. What was there to lose? She wasn't bad looking either.

Eve had taken the last sip of her first drink. 'I'm not really a Scotch drinker — I'm more of a G&T kind of girl. But when in hardship, this will do. Another?' She put her hand out to her arm's length and he obeyed by pouring another drink.

'I'm not normally a crier but it's been a long day. San Wu is not what I expected. Is he alright, do you think?' She had her head down and was looking at the photo. As she said this to Josefo, she looked up with warm, fluid eyes and saw a man she hardly knew. She let the glass drop to the floor, slipped off the side of the bed and walked the two steps to his chair. She looked down at him and as he was about to respond, she moved herself on top of his body to sit facing him, thighs across his hips, knees finding their place and her face level with his. She had not looked at him so closely before but could now see perfect, brown eyes and a mouth far too ready to pluck. She put her mouth on his and lost herself in his lips and the warmth of his tongue stealing what tenderness was left in the normal coldness of his heart. He closed his eyes and found himself in a world he could not lead, and was happy to submit to an adversary so willing to take command. He felt a warmth rise up in him that he had not experienced in a long time. It was more than lust, he didn't recognize it. It was something unknown to him. He kept his eyes closed and drew her lips into his. Their tongues touched and danced in the moistness of their joined flesh, first flat then pointed, darting up and down, forward and back, frolicking in the darkness of heat. He felt the familiar stirring in his groin, almost painful with the pressure building in his head and veins.

He didn't know what hit him.

37

He lay on his bed looking at the ceiling of his hut with Eve's diary in his left hand. He felt the texture of its cover as his eyes continued to watch the ceiling with the walls fading in and out of focus. Alcohol had never had a good effect on him and he wondered why he had consumed so much. It had seemed a good idea at the time. It slurred his speech and blurred the edges of reason. It distracted him and slowed down his brain. He needed his brain to be quick, not delayed in an alcoholic blur. He wondered how long it would take her to realize he had the diary and what she would do. This woman had revealed many sides of herself he had never expected to discover that night in the rain. She drank, she cried, she loved her dead father, and she lost control. He wasn't surprised by the first few things he'd discovered about her. But to find out she was a sensual and assertive woman was unbelievable. He smiled at the memory. He had not experienced anything like it. His brain wallowed in the alcoholic pain of the aftertaste but he still remembered the night, the sweet meeting of their two bodies in a sweaty connection of souls, sharing an experience neither had expected, nor would forget. Even the memory of it now, several hours later, made his palms sweat and his blood pump more quickly to his still unfocused brain. He remembered her smooth skin in the darkness of the room and his own skin dark and driven, not above her but beneath, at her mercy, her will and her want. It didn't seem right a woman being like this, confident, striving, grasping to get her own pleasure. And yet it was pleasurable even though he had not experienced it before. He felt it wasn't wrong and needed to be there again. Only one thing bothered him about that night. It wasn't the diary. He had succeeded at that task, he thought proudly looking at it in his hand, flicking its pages with the other. That was just a stepping stone to his ambition. It was something else he was anxious about, increasing the moisture in his sweaty palms and further pulsating his racing heart. He had lost control and in that loss he had said something to her that he had never uttered to any woman in his life. All he hoped was she had not heard his soft voice in the awakening of their passion. He hoped she would never know what was unravelling in his heart.

He had not known love — true love — with a woman. He had felt something in the past while making love with the women he met and with the joining of their bodies but this feeling had always ended when he left. He did not know these women as people with opinions. This time was different. Eve was now a friend, someone he cared about, and would fight for. Most of his fighting was for money, feelings had nothing to do with it, merely a carrying out of instructions from a higher authority. Some structures were there for a reason and if unbalanced would affect the stability of the ecosystem of which he was an important part. He had felt the other side of love — the yearning and pain of love missing, like a piece of him gone wandering in the wilderness needing to be found and nurtured. This love he knew well but it was a different kind of love, one that never left him.

He felt a twinge of pain as he looked at the diary in his hand. He didn't read it, feeling that he would be breaking a code of honor, reading a person's private thoughts not meant for him. Stealing it was a different matter and did not fall into the category of deceit or betrayal. He was just doing what was asked, nothing more, nothing less. The slight pain he felt in his chest, however, did not subside as he slipped the diary in a secret hole between the mattress cover and the old mattress itself. He took several deep breaths as he reached into his coat pocket and finished off the last of the alcohol left in the bottle consumed earlier in the evening. It was nearly morning and he had left her semiconscious and comfortable in her bed to await the morning light. She would awaken without him and wonder if it had all been a dream. Or so he hoped as he closed his eyes.

38

That sick feeling came upon him as he handed over the diary to San Wu. There had not been many times in Josefo's life recently when he didn't experience that feeling but he knew it had not always been with him. He remembered his youth on the farm with his dogs and beloved sister and knew that he had once been good. Some time after his 16th birthday, the sick feeling started. It was only recently, since meeting this foreign woman that he had felt its relentless grip again playing with his mind and his heart. It didn't belong there — he had no remorse, there was no room for it in the endless row of days he called his life. If he were meant to trust people, something called God would have made everyone nice. But that was not how it was, nor could it ever be. People were not to be trusted — like for like. He would give no trust and receive none in return.

There was another sensation he could not budge. He was surprised and angry at first that it had thrust itself upon him. This thing he had successfully cast from his life a long time ago and intended never to appear again. He knew its name. Most people called it love but how did it appear to him? Love was something you felt for your dogs or parents or sister. But to feel this for a person about your own age, and a foreigner at that? This was inconceivable. He had never loved a woman.

But this woman had brought upon him feelings he had not experienced. She had taken him body and soul and now he could not shift her image from his mind — this troubled, small foreigner had subsumed him, entered his bloodstream and was infecting his very life force. He felt it in his stomach, his head, his heart. He didn't like it, yet yearned for her like no other person or thing that had gone before.

*

San Wu gripped the book with an unusual force and Josefo could see a burning behind the older man's eyes that was frightening. He had been frightened before by this man but he had never been close enough to see his eyes. His position was growing in importance and his actions were testament to his courage.

'You are serving me well. You will soon be the new force for the party. Just be patient, my son.' San Wu had never used Josefo's name so he was not sure whether he knew or remembered it. A minor concern when the great man paid him such compliments.

Josefo left the great hall as he had done before. Way up on his left as he made his way back to his hut, he could see Eve on the hill allotment San Wu had provided for her. She had turned her head at the same time and their eyes met briefly. She had turned again to get back to monitoring her hill workers and hadn't looked back.

He couldn't go on avoiding her like this. He knew he had to face her soon enough. He decided it was up to him to make the move.

39

Before she opened her eyes, Eve could taste the dryness in her mouth. She knew by the heat of day penetrating the walls of the hut that it was late morning. She began to move in bed until she realized her whole body ached, not just her head. She opened her eyes but closed them again at the brightness of the light coming through the curtains.

There was a commotion outside, understandable when she realized it was close to noon. Most inhabitants of town were up at 6 am. She was about to roll over and go back to sleep when she remembered.

It came flashing back to her in a blur, a fragmented experience like a flickering image extinguished by the burning film. But the image did not disappear, it lingered in her mind and stayed there, swaying before it closed in on reality. It seemed unreal to her, she was the actress in an adventure film who took events into her own hands. But it was her. Eve — conservative, submissive Eve who had not been with a man since Roger had packed his bags after impregnating someone else. Should she look for the husk of self she had shed that night to prove she had emerged as someone different?

The pleasure was still hovering, a tangible thing that wanted to stick around. She would let it. She had never invited it in but it had managed to shanghai her friendship with a man she didn't even know she could trust.

She wasn't sorry or ashamed as she may have been in another time and place. The normal anxiety around her sexuality, as everything else in her life, had disappeared last night, the first time she was able to test its power of survival. Not only was it gone but it had been replaced with a love of body and self that translated into a deep inner pleasure she had never experienced. The ultimate climax had been with a man she did not know, love or welcome to her soul as she had always believed it must. What a revelation! She didn't dwell on it for long as she thought it would be a single event she would not dive into again. Her body tingled at the memory of his touch.

She opened her eyes to the day, pushed her hand under the mattress and felt around for the small, hard-backed book she returned there every night and reached for every morning. But this morning her fingers did not meet the familiar cover of the only remaining link to her father's memory. The diary was gone and there was only one person who could have taken it. She struggled to remember the order of events of the night before and when she had last seen the diary but the blood kept rushing to her head every time his image appeared.

Perhaps he had just borrowed it, intending to bring it back today. Should she wait and see what transpired? Or should she assume that this had been the primary purpose of his visit and feel used and betrayed by this accomplice of the devil. Yet, even if she wanted to she could not think of Josefo as evil — she couldn't feel it in him. And she always trusted her instincts.

She walked to the bathroom with squat toilet she had not yet become used to, washed her face trying to avoid movement to her head, cleaned her teeth and dragged herself into the shower. She deliberated the best way to get the diary back or find out its whereabouts, without getting herself killed. She knew this was a very real option. She dried off and pulled on her well-worn camouflage pants and green singlet followed by her white calico shirt as a final covering.

She heard footsteps at the door and then knocking. What if it was Josefo? Should she be angry or should she play ignorant at first to see what would happen? She opened the door but it was not Josefo who greeted her. One of the young soldiers she had seen around the compound was standing at the door informing her that San Wu was ready for another audience.

'Please come now, Miss.'

She was hurried off and this time she had nothing to bring but herself.

She started the long walk up to the main building and cast a sideways glance as she passed Josefo's hut. She saw no life inside so she headed up the hill, a repeat performance of the night before which seemed so long ago.

She wondered if this was normal practice to be seeing San Wu so soon after having waited so long. She supposed there was no routine as he did seem slightly eccentric — even in this part of the world. Her head was clearing by the step but she still had a thirst to quench. She motioned to the young soldier, putting her hand to her mouth like a cup hoping he would understand. He offered her a sip of water from his flask and the dryness left her throat.

She approached the large doors which opened suddenly and she was greeted by the long red carpet.

This time San Wu was already sitting on his throne, looking straight ahead at Eve as she entered the hall. There was no sound as she walked on the carpet while the young soldier accompanying her was the only guard present. Eve and San Wu were alone.

As she approached him seated on his throne, she saw that she was now privileged to have a proper chair to sit on directly opposite San Wu on the podium, at the same level.

The guard helped her up the stairs and as she was climbing she caught a glimpse of the pink slippers San Wu chose as an adornment for his feet. She sat down in the chair which was comfortable and which molded well against her body. She looked at San Wu.

'Good morning, Eve. I trust you slept well after our talk yesterday.' He gave a half smile as he looked down the length of her body from her eyes to her toes. She didn't like the feeling.

'I had an unsettled night — there were many emotions going through my heart and head as you may imagine.' She wondered if he could imagine or at least remember what it was like to make love to another human being.

'Ah yes — young Josefo. He's a good soldier — this I know. As a man, that is another question! I have a surprise for you.' San Wu rabbit-hopped and brought his legs up underneath him, then propelled himself into the air and landed on the velvet cushion with his feet. At the same time, he squealed in a high-pitched voice which reverberated one-hundred-fold around the auditorium, producing an eerie chorus of himself multiplied. Now, standing on his chair, he grabbed something from inside his jacket and waved it in front of Eve.

'I have it! Ha! I told you I would have it the next

time we met. I was right — you were wrong! Ha!' He looked to Eve as if he were going to dance with glee like Rumpelstiltskin. And, thought Eve, like that ancient rotund gnome, his personality could change at any moment. She couldn't mistake what he held in front of her — the now dog-eared diary, well-thumbed and read from cover to cover.

'You see — what do you think?' he asked.

'Where did you get that? You must have had someone steal it. Who is the thief?'

'Let us just say that I arranged for it to be borrowed. Do not blame the boy — it was not his fault. He was just carrying out orders. There is no refusal, you know.'

Eve didn't want to ponder on that but started thinking about her leverage and what he had found out that had been revealed in the diary. At least she was the angry one, not San Wu. She had begun to understand it was always better when he was smiling and jovial, however demented he appeared.

'You have it now, what did you learn?' Eve was gaining confidence, her head was clearing and the tiredness was disappearing.

'All interesting. All I knew anyway but this person who wrote these words has filled in some detail. I will tell you more later. I will keep the diary. Go now. Goodbye. And do not forget the boy.'

Eve was about to protest that he was hardly a boy when the guard appeared in front of her and said: 'Miss, you must come with me now. San Wu must rest.'

The excitement had been overwhelming for him and as she was escorted along the red carpet, she turned to see him being lifted from the throne, coughing, his back bent over as he shuffled off the dais behind the curtain and into darkness.

40

The next morning Eve was awake with the sun. After dressing, she walked up to the hillside just past the perimeter of the village and looked out across the valley. She was standing at the pinnacle of a hill, to one side she could look down and see the village with small huts dotted on either side of the mounds, to the other, field after field of plants taller than humans carrying their loads of lethal cargo.

Eve had been given an allotment of land of her own to sow and rear the magic babies that would be her freedom. If she could pull it off.

It had been a generous gift to her from San Wu — five hectares of rich arable hillside land ready to accept the fecund seed that would provide a new marketable product and wealth to the community. Or so she had promised. She looked at the dimensions of the plot, jotted down a few calculations in a notebook and thought, casting her mind back to her student days when they were given sample plots and various tasks to complete within a timeframe. It was a simple enough procedure: one she had undertaken many times in her studies and since then in her work. The Australian land was a lot less rich and the soil completely different — as were the species of plants. But the process would be the same. Calculating the timings would be different and would need a trial run with control groups to gather comparative data.

The land had been cleared of any existing plant life. As she stood at the edge of the area, she looked across at the next field and could see plants as high as herself weighed down by the heaviness of giant green opium pods, almost ripe for the plucking. Standing amidst the birthplace of the catalyst for death, she decided she needed to be committed to the deal. She would not let herself judge whether this decision was good or bad, she was here and she had to see it through.

She had played her hand and now had to play out the game. Playing it out meant working harder than she ever had before, even with such an immovable incentive.

Her days unfolded from dawn to sundown measuring, cataloguing, germinating the seeds and saplings. It was a constant round of tracking the ground, her team working hard by her side.

Several weeks passed and her long structured days were taking their toll on her body. She was bone weary, with aching arms and back at the end of each day of continual bending and rising. Only once did she glimpse a figure standing on his balcony high above the men's quarters still wearing his pink slippers.

The constant toil of her work took all of her mind. It was only once in those first days and weeks that she thought of Josefo and realized she had not seen him since their night together. She had thought hard about what had happened and knew that what she missed most about him was what was so difficult to get from him, his companionship and the connection of two souls. Each night as she walked back to her dwelling, she wondered where he was. There was no sign of life in his hut.

41

'Alex was a carefree fun-loving child, a sportsman, attractive to both males and females and while not excelling at school because of his social activities, he was a good student and lover of knowledge. He had been unaware of his father's growing reputation, preferring to indulge in his studies and his friendships with Dottmar and Ko Tan. I used to watch him from a distance when I was Raoul's assistant and began to resent his life of privilege and the inheritance he was one day certain to receive. Raoul used to tell me he worried about Alex becoming like a lot of the expat children — not focused, too much into social exploits, too much wealth, and not hungry enough. He wanted Alex to understand that not everyone was as lucky as he and make him yearn to be involved in the lives of others.'

San Wu paused. Eve was crouched in her usual spot, not uncomfortable though her legs had started to lose feeling. She was used to this and ignored the pain for as long as she could. San Wu had called an audience after her first field work and she was more than ready to hear his words.

'At 15, Raoul removed Alex from his beloved

boarding school and installed him at home once more. Alex loved his aya. His mother had left when he was born so his aya was like the mother he had never known. She had not tried to take his mother's place — merely to be a friend and mentor to the boy with the white blond hair. Her heart nearly burst when she had to say goodbye to him that first time. Each subsequent time after the end of school holidays she hoped the pain would ease — but it did not. When she heard that he was coming home for good, she was whole again.

Alex on the other hand, was not happy to be coming home two years early. He had pleaded with his father and refused to leave his friends. His father would not be swayed, however, and knew Alex would see his friends at day school anyway. Raoul's decision was made. We developed a kind of friendship, Alex and I. The boy looked up to me in his way and yet also patronized me, I felt. I kept my distance but always harbored a profound sense of envy for this easy-come, easy-go boy. I knew in my heart he would never make a leader.'

San Wu stopped and clapped his hands. He jumped to his feet and jogged around the spacious room making soft squelching sounds with his felt-covered slippers. He raised his arms above his head and then twirled them from side to side, jogged back and recovered his place on the gold velvet cushion opposite Eve without uttering a word.

'The leader of the military government, Poi Trang, was not happy with the growing reputation of the unnamed one, this British expat known as the Tiger. He was determined to find out his identity and stop him from spreading his organization that presumed to question the government. This rogue group had become an annoyance and the intelligence gathering they continued to undertake was now too much to bear. Poi Trang had a country to run — he did not need some foreigner sticking his nose in where the local people did not want it. He did not understand the ways of this country and its people. They did not want independence — they needed a leader to guide them where they had to be led. Raoul and Poi Trang had more than the tug of freedom to fight over. Poi Trang had a new mistress, the former wife of Raoul and mother to Alex, Alexandra. A woman holding the affection of two men is a not a pretty sight, Eve. She used her womanly disposition to be wholly disloyal, not only to a man, but to a family. This I could not forgive her for. But who was she to me? You may well ask me this. She was no one. But a disloyal woman is never to be trusted. Raoul somehow managed to forget this. It would be his downfall.

'Poi Trang eventually traced Raoul to his jungle headquarters. It was not only Freedom Party members who remembered the secret meeting place in the jungle. His former wife had an excellent memory regarding romantic rendezvous locations in the happy days of her marriage. The raid was at night, of course, and took the group by surprise. A few of the men were able to warn Raoul who fled the camp and escaped into the night. But it was not Poi Trang who followed Raoul relentlessly and finally wore him down, corralled him into a valley and shot him in the head. Alex heard the shot but the others would not let him follow the sounds. It was only at dawn when he sneaked out and found his father's broken body in the creek at the bottom of the embankment. Alex never knew who pulled the trigger.

'Who was it?' Eve asked.

'I cannot say,' was all San Wu offered.

'Alex was devastated. He had come to know his father only in those last two years — had grown to love and respect him. But I also was grieving. I had lost the only father I had known. The Freedom Party members threw the leader's cap at Alex and told him he had inherited the right to take over from his father. He had proved himself in their eyes. I was older, wiser, stronger, a better fighter — all of these things meant nothing in the face of blood. He was the son, not the son elect. He would always win.

'Alex took the reins under duress. He did not think he was leadership material and did not want to replace his father's memory. However, as time went on he gained the respect of the party and gradually grew in confidence. By the time he was 20 he was a proud and dignified leader of men prepared to risk his own life for the cause he had grown to respect and love. But it would not last.'

42

Papa Chau Lap looked around at the handful of townsfolk who had arrived in the low-lying village. Only a small number had survived the long walk and his heart was weighed down with disappointment. This grew to a deep sadness when he looked at the allotment of land he had been given by the government and the seeds to sow. It was not rice that was to be farmed here. After being pushed off their own land and told of riches to be had in low-lying rice paddies, they were now faced with farming the evil seed they had so longed to avoid — the poppy. The other settlers told him they had tried growing rice but it was only suited to the mountainous jungle regions not the dry flatlands. He raised his eyes from the ground, heedless of the steadily pouring rain, hopeful of seeing his son.

He imagined the tall young man still beside him as he had been every day for the last three months. He had been a support to his father when they buried his sister just dead from dysentery. It was a far different hole from the one dug only weeks before. But Papa Chau Lap's son was not with him when he reached his destination, the end they had worked toward for so long.

Only two days before arriving, he had fallen dead at his father's feet. The first job Papa had to do in his new home was bury his oldest son.

Papa Chau Lap's family was gone, and he had no crop. For three months he had motivated the others, urged them not to give up hope, telling them of the new lives, new inspiration that would be waiting. Who would motivate him now? All energy was spent. He sat on the dry ground in some clothes that had been allocated to him. The bundles allocated to his wife and two children lay next to him — untouched in their bags roped together.

How was he to start over again with no family, love or incentive to keep him going? What would be the reason? Why should he try? There was no hope or reason to continue. He picked his aching body off the ground, wiped the dirt off his pants and carried the bundles of clothes into the small hut given to him by the government. He opened the door and walked into the room. A makeshift wooden bed occupied the middle of the room, with two children's beds on one side. A large bucket sat next to the wall. He placed the bundle of clothes on the bed, lingering to look at the items of clothing his wife and children would never wear, and walked back out to the waiting poppy field.

43

Blue sky tempered the grey these days, the clouds were frightened away only to reappear later in the day when it was safe to make an appearance. The rain would come, expectedly, every afternoon, but not long and heavy as it had been. It was now light rain easily persuaded to make a short visit.

This blue day was a good omen or so Josefo thought. He lived his life and made his choices by the whims of the weather. He was looking out of his hut window seeing the clear sky and hearing the early morning ramblings of the birds who had overslept. The track up the hill was almost dry and the village was coming alive. He turned his head in the direction of the hilltop on the edge of the settlement. There were moving black figures with straw hats bent over in deference to the day, he thought. His eyes darted from one figure to another until he stopped and focused on one lighter figure moving among the darker ones. His eyes stayed there as he began to dress, pulling on his boots and checking his equipment.

His eyes watched his feet place themselves one in front of the other in the relentless pursuit of the track. He only looked up once or twice merely to ensure his bearing was correct, to adjust and progress. The gradient steepened and he adjusted his body to the slope as the soles of his boots clung to the gravelly road which turned into softer soil. As he reached the crest of the hill and her allotment, he saw ahead of him the darkened forms which were clearly the figures of the Burmese workers allocated to Eve by San Wu, saw their heads briefly rise and then look down again to continue sowing. The light figure in the background came into view and Josefo stopped in front of her, her former pale features now darkened by the sun. She looked up at him with a wry, almost amused expression he didn't understand. He reached out his hand to touch her fingers. They did not recoil from his touch, her smallest finger slightly curving to the shape of his own.

'I have missed you. I do not want to miss you again.' At his words, she smiled into his eyes, letting her other four fingers wrap themselves around his hand.

44

The heat intensified even in the mountains where it was a few degrees cooler than the coast. The rains had come and the soil was moist for most of the day and wet again after the night rain. The soil had become water logged with patches of boggy wet clay that was difficult to handle. Canals had to be dug to allow the water to run off from the new crop which was into its second month of life. Eve was taking no risks and was adding to her notes daily about progress, shape and form, every detail was recorded for analysis. She was pleased with the development of its growth — 'it' she could not yet describe. It was new with no name or past but she was compelled to allow it a future. How it would differ from the current poppy she didn't know, but she did know there was something magical about this new seed she had created from several different sources. Propagation had been one of her strong subjects at university and she had a vast knowledge of the outcomes of mixing different seed families. But those were Australian seed families. This one she knew little about.

It had been her last year of university; the final testing year which would identify the best students for continuing research work. Her marks were in the top ten and she was shortlisted for a research doctorate. She had been studying, her hours long. Roger had been supportive for most of her schooling but something had changed. He was no longer happy with her continuing her education. He needed to see an end. He had other plans for them both, plans that Eve had ignored in preference to her work, even if it was unpaid. Her propagation research was funded and was reaping results, but these were not the results Roger wanted for himself, for his own family. He wanted a baby and, it seemed, was not prepared to wait for her to be ready. How could she contemplate such a thought when she was in the full swing of a research grant that could be taken away at any time? It was the one point they argued about.

'Eve, I can't wait forever. You have to make your choice.' And so she had made her choice, one she would forever regret.

He left one warm September day and she found herself living her life alone.

45

Eve looked down at the rich soil that was the home of her new fruit. She held out her hands and noticed the long slender fingers caked with dirt she found impossible to remove. The creases on the inside of her palms formed rivers of age. Her lifeline was cut sharply in half. The lines definite and clear but distinctly separate before and after a point in her life that was blank — the missing piece that couldn't bridge the two joins. However, the line continued on its healthy route, long and down almost into her wrist. At a local market in Australia, an old gypsy woman had told her it was a sign of very long life and good health. The woman knew this from the rules of reading and her intuitive spirits. But what of the gap in her lifeline? The woman had held her hand so strongly it hurt, her eyes buried in her palm.

'This gap is life gone, Miss. But not forgotten.'

The world of riddles did not entertain her. She paid the woman and left. Halfway through her life would come a change. This she could accept and certainly, in retrospect, this had proven to be true. She saw that line now, not quite obscured by the dirt of the hill. More lines had grown into her hand. She wondered if hands aged with lines in the same way as the lines on the face.

46

Mya scurried off to answer the banging on the front door of the house.

When she re-appeared on the terrace, she was followed by two Burmese policemen; one in uniform, the other in plain clothes.

'May we please speak to the parents of Abau?' The plain clothes policeman spoke just as Dottmar and Ko Tan were rising to greet them.

'Oh no, what has happened?'

'We are his parents,' Ko Tan managed to say.

'I am Inspector Dau and this is Detective Sergeant Muntu. I am afraid your son is dead — found murdered with a knife wound to the neck. He was found in a shallow ditch at the side of the old Rangoon Road. Not a pretty sight. You — one of you — must come and identify the body. What is left of it. It looks as if the body has been there for some time.'

The Burmese police were not well known for their subtlety but more for their reluctance to get to the point.

Dottmar slumped into a chair, sobbing, holding her head in her hands. Ko Tan was almost white, all blood drained from his face leaving him lifeless and silent.

'My beautiful son ...' It would be some time before he would be able to let the tears fall.

The second policeman, Muntu, now spoke, Dau having taken a seat pondering the croissants at breakfast.

'What do you know of an Eve Robinson — a woman from Australia?' He was less abrupt than Dau, though his eyes were no less harsh.

'She is my ...' Dottmar began, '... friend from Australia who is here on holiday. What of it?' Ko Tan stood over the first policeman and looked the second in the eye.

'We have reason to believe she was the last person to be seen with your son alive. We have witnesses — and we have spoken to the embassy. There are records of her movements.' The bad cop stopped speaking and eyed the croissants lovingly until he motioned to Ko Tan, 'May I?' Ko Tan snorted.

'I think I know what you are suggesting, Inspector and it is a very serious accusation.' Ko Tan almost spat out the words.

Dau delicately placed the croissant in his mouth and closed his eyes.

'Good breakfast. So where is this woman now? Can we speak to her, find out her side of the story? You said she was staying here with you.' He shuffled in his seat as he rubbed his hands together to rid himself of the crumbs from the croissant.

Dottmar removed her hands from her face and looked at Ko Tan with red, watery eyes.

'I am sorry to tell you that we have a warrant to search the house,' Dau rose and made his way to the door. 'Please ...?'

Dottmar and Ko Tan knew better than to obstruct police business. They led the two men to Eve's room first. They had a cursory look inside, Dau writing something in his notebook. Muntu pulled open the wardrobe, had a cursory glimpse and they both walked out of the room.

'Your son's room?' Dottmar led the way to Abau's room up the corridor. They hadn't touched the room since they had first known he was missing.

Dau spoke first. 'You have known your son was missing. Why did you not report this to us?' Ko Tan looked awkwardly at Dottmar and after some time spoke.

'We thought we knew where he was, and would be able to find him. We never realized he was in danger. I was so terribly wrong!'

'Yes. It was not wise.' Muntu went again to Abau's wardrobe, pulled on the handle. The door stayed shut.

'You have the key for this?' He asked Dottmar the question.

'Abau kept all his own keys. Let me see.' She opened a couple of the desk drawers, flicked over the contents, and closed the drawers with empty hands. 'I can find no key here.'

'I must ...' Muntu motioned a pulling action, nodding. Dottmar also nodded and looked to the floor. He continued the motion, placed one foot on one side of the wardrobe and gave a strong pull. The wardrobe was made of light wood so it gave way easily, taking the lock with it. Inside was Eve's backpack.

Dottmar let out a moan. 'Eve's things! Ko Tan, what has happened to her?' Ko Tan darted an angry look at Dottmar.

'She is also missing and Abau has her kitbag in his room. This is not good. She is either dead or responsible for his death. Either way, she is in big trouble.'

Ko Tan regained confidence. 'She is an Australian citizen so you will have to go through her embassy for any investigation. I suggest you follow procedure.'

Muntu passed a look to his colleague who began making his way to the corridor leading to the front entrance.

'And so we shall. Be prepared for us again, Sir.' They walked the length of the corridor and left as they had entered, this time with Mya following.

Dottmar watched Mya saying goodbye to the men at the door. She seemed to be taking longer than necessary but when she shut the door she came running back to the terrace.

'Ko Tan, we have to find Eve and warn her if she is still in the city. She couldn't have been involved in this, surely not. Who can we get to help?' Dottmar implored Ko Tan.

'One of my trusted men can find her. I am sure of it. Wherever she is, Dottmar, do not worry, we must and we will find her first.'

Mya stayed close to Ko Tan and decided she would have the final say as to what would happen to the Australian.

47

San Wu released his grip on the man's neck and let his body fall to the ground. The peasant leader lay prostrate in the dirt surrounded by the foreigner's 'hyperplant'. She had done well for someone new to this place, for a while anyway. Led him to think she knew how to grow the opium poppy bigger and better than crop farmers who had been growing it for centuries. But now he knew the truth. She had been growing tobacco, that common seed worthless in the current market. She had grown healthy strong plants that, from his distant eyrie, held a similarity to the poppy in the early stages of growth. It was her confidence and the knowledge she exhibited that soon needed proof. He needed to come out of his lair and prove she could do it. She had tricked him. How had he fallen for this lie and let her get away with this for months all the time giving her the information she so desired? Just because she had book learning about plants from a western country? Is that why he had been fooled so easily? Or was it because she was the Tiger's granddaughter, related to his mentor, the man he trusted and loved? He had kept himself indoors for too long, he realized that now. He should have stifled those urges to be alone, should have forced himself to monitor and watch what was going on in the village. He would no longer be a hermit wallowing in past glory. He would continue to lead, relive the glory days when he created this community, and sustained its people on the nectar of the gods. He needed no successor, he had found new energy, a new vigor to lead. Disappointment would come to the intended 2IC. San Wu knew how to deal with him.

As he made his way out of his gilded cage through the village to the crop on the hill early that morning, the sight that met his eyes sickened his stomach. Dirty tobacco. And the dirty peasant leader following her instructions, showing disloyalty to his leader, knew the path he was taking. He never stood a chance and almost gave himself to San Wu as his deserved fate. San Wu had not killed for a long time, viewed it as a duty of the past not often required since he had such well-trained deputies. It was a spur of the moment thing, a flashback from a former time when he was unable to control his innate urges. He had forgotten how strong his hands and arms were, they were still capable of crushing a man's neck and throat within seconds. He calculated it would take less than two minutes from the time he had his hands around the peasant's neck, to expiration of breath and death. The man had not struggled, it was easy, as it had always been. It was too tiring for him to kill the rest of the peasants working on this crop of deceit. He ordered two of his bodyguards to gather the group out of sight over the hill and execute them. The Australian woman could wait. He did not tolerate deception, she had to pay the highest price.

San Wu took to the plants. He grabbed the stem and root and pulled at each, disrupting the ground, leaving open graves of earth no longer requiring life. Grinding his teeth and dribbling spit, he forced his way through half the yield, destroying everything at arm's length. Exhausted at last, he called his deputies to do the rest and walked back to his retreat, spent.

San Wu looked back at her so-called hyper crop now uprooted and homeless, their lifeless forms lying in alphabet shapes amidst the rifled dirt, and knew that the woman would never again be blessed with his conversation. Her time had passed, she could help him no more. It was a shame. He'd begun to like her.

48

They had moved into a large hut and were living as a couple, one of few in the village. Eve was surprised San Wu had allowed them this privilege but it was Josefo who had been summoned that time to accept the offering, and one so generous. She didn't take him for someone blessing a couple and offering them privacy. She wondered what had prompted it, but continued to concentrate on her work and life with Josefo.

At first they were stared at and, Eve was sure, Josefo felt compelled to provide explanations to the other young soldiers in camp. But soon the furtive looks and sly smiles were gone, and they began to settle into life with each other. Every day she learned more about him; his likes and dislikes, wants and habits. Not all were pleasant but she knew men well enough to know that most had bad habits they never wanted to admit to. She came to realize she was happy.

They had a small dining room in their quarters where Josefo prepared local meals of rice and meat enhanced with Burmese and Indian spices. After early dinners, they would stroll up to the hillside to check on the crops in the moonlight, looking out for the silhouettes of the ever-watchful sentries. Nothing man-made would destroy these crops she knew, but she did not trust nature. It was the vagaries of nature that most-often spoiled the hard work and solid hours of toil of horticulturists. She had experienced this frustration and pain many times. She had learned that, through planning, destruction could be minimized and she took precautions in her crop rotation process and seeding techniques. As they walked up to the hill each night, Josefo would slowly touch her hand and bring it up to his lips, brushing her fingers with the warmth of his breath. But he did not dare to ask the question on his lips.

Her toil had rewarded her well, the plants were bountiful and, true to her word, were growing twice as fast and as large as San Wu's plants on the other side of the hill. She was confident he would be impressed by the growth from his distant perch and would not see the detail in the plants themselves. As she and Josefo walked back down the hill to their hut, she was satisfied that it would not be long before she could reveal her success. She had not thought through how it would be revealed, but she would have to act quickly.

She had thought long about the loss of her diary. In itself, the diary was something tangible she could refer to, a memory of her father. She had read the contents over and over and realized there was nothing in it that could be detrimental to her or even informative for San Wu. He knew so much more than its contents. And was willing to tell her, it seemed. It concerned her that Josefo had stolen it, but she knew she did not understand the ways of this community. His ambition was strong, she couldn't deny that. His life was so different from hers. Loyalty was different here; obeisance unlike that in Australia. There, the people questioned first, children learned not to obey, but to query, research, find out and follow if it suited them. It was different in this country, in the mountains. She knew she would never understand it, or him. All she knew was that she wanted to be with him for now. The future she could not determine.

The next morning, they rose early; Josefo to organize a dawn reconnaissance and Eve to visit the crop. San Wu had planned for Josefo to lead a small team into the breaking day to investigate some claims of border activity the night before. Eve shouted good luck to him as she made her way to the high ground where the sun was peeping over its rounded head.

She had not expected what greeted her this morning. Safety had never been a concern, not forceful, purposeful destruction. It was nature she had always been wary of. She surveyed the hilltop from one side to the other and decided that no silent storm in the night could have wreaked such devastation on her growing children. Not only was every plant pulled out of the ground by its roots but each one was sliced, with hundreds of growing seeds gone. The ground was littered with the fragile scraps of tattered leaves and stems half shaved and half chopped from their dusty homes. As she stood in shock on the hillside, she became aware that no workers were turning up as they usually did each morning at 5. Could this be related to the dawn patrol. Could they somehow have known this was to happen? Her pulse raced at the thought of all the hours and months of work that would bear no fruit until she thought of Josefo. She felt her head go dizzy as she turned and ran back down the hill to a group of soldiers in the compound.

49

It was not usual for San Wu to ask Josefo to patrol at dawn. Josefo had spent many of his early years under the command of soldiers doing this very task, patrolling by day and night, venturing beyond the boundaries of his existence, seeing life as no one should see it and returning against his will. The times varied, but the task was the same; seek out and kill and, if that was not possible, maim.

The patrols were often successful and had kept the marauding gangs away from the precious enclave that was home at the time. But now he was being lined up as the successor to a great man who had put his trust in a young soldier to take over the reins. Why then, did he get given this grunt work, fit only for an inexperienced, untested soldier? He was beyond this mundanity, he deserved a higher goal. These early mornings were only fit for the foot soldiers, not worthy of someone being groomed to rule. San Wu had been insistent and was not responsive to an opposing view. Josefo accepted the job, with the hope that this would lead to more fulfilling tasks, tasks that would call on his leadership and strategic thinking.

The walk out to the rendezvous point had been uneventful and the jungle track clear of threat. Still,

Josefo was suspicious and his gut told him the same thing — be wary. He couldn't say why he felt suspicious, he had covered this track many times, knew the country like his own skin, its undulations, thickets and boulders had been his home for years. His patrol was solid, men he had known for ten or more years, trusted companions as well as highly competent fighters.

Josefo gathered the other five men and navigated them to a point on the border where San Wu told him he had heard reports of skirmishes. Josefo had no details of these skirmishes, he had taken San Wu's word for it. Why question the great man? His expertise had been honed on military tactics Josefo had only begun to learn. San Wu would prove to be a valuable mentor.

When his small squad approached the area, there was no evidence to suggest any border activity apart from some wild pigs and prolific birdlife. It was a short patrol by comparison to many others he had done — only a two-hour trek to the border and back. An easy patrol, on a pleasant day with no rain yet. He knew any reconnaissance could be fruitless but this one seemed to him to be wasteful of his time and talents and noted to himself to speak to San Wu about the continuing wrongful use of his skills. He preferred to participate at the higher strategic level, to be involved in the planning stages more suited to his new status.

Josefo signaled the order to inspect the border, noting any discrepancies for his report. However, there was nothing of significance to add.

'Come on everyone. We will head south. There's nothing to be found here. The area is clear.'

The men turned to follow him as he checked his direction and readjusted his backpack and ammunition belt. As usual he was in visual contact with the man behind. The soldier at point, as lookout, was well ahead, while Josefo commanded from the middle of the group.

He saw the point soldier running towards him.

'Sir, the peasant farmers are ahead!'

'What are they doing out here?' The point soldier shook his head just as Eve's team of workers came into view through the foliage.

'Josefo!' The first peasant shouted at Josefo, his arms flailing, the other peasants trying to catch up behind him.

'What's going on — you should get back to the crop. There are possible skirmishes ahead!'

'San Wu killed our lead farmer! He ordered his two deputies to kill us but I bribed him into saving us.'

The explosion hurt their ears. The initial reaction of the men trained in combat, was to hit the ground, making themselves as flat as possible, burying their faces in the dirt. Josefo was stunned out of his complacency by the assault on his ears and body. He had hit the ground like the others and checked around the area to see where the men had dived amidst the noise. He turned and spotted two of them behind him on the left.

Josefo called out to the man ahead. 'Au Ku — are you alive?' There was no reply. He snaked along the ground, his equipment brushing up against the rocks and uneven turf below him. He didn't have far to crawl before he saw the pieces of red flesh on the ground and hanging from the bushes. Crawling forward, he reached the remains of the soldier who never saw it coming. The stench of death was already present, he knew it well.

'Pu Kay, Au Kung, Ho Tan — keep down.' Even though he sensed his team members were dead, his resolve was to keep the group cohesive, just in case. He didn't want to accept that he was the last to survive.

He lay hugging the ground for some time, quiet,

listening. When there was quiet, he lifted his head up and looked over his shoulder. There was no sound so the perpetrators had probably gone, assuming the members of the patrol were all dead. There was always the threat of land mines, which was what he thought killed most of his comrades; certainly the soldier at point.

Josefo maneuvered his body backwards covering as much ground as he could. This proved too difficult so he turned around 180 degrees and faced the shredded bodies of the dead, bodies that would never see a venerated funeral pyre. No death was pretty and he never got used to it. Who could the perpetrators have been? Or had it been landmines? He attempted to cover the bodies with twigs, sticks and leaves and to provide at least some privacy for the men in death. He couldn't do much for Au Ku who had borne the brunt of the attack at the front of the patrol. He would have to remain in pieces, for the birds. His family would never need to know.

Aware that he was now on his own, and probably surrounded by unfriendly forces, Josefo checked his weapon and ammo stocks. Still good. Even though he heard no sound, it was not wise to assume safety. He had learnt the hard way, thinking it was all clear, he had been shot in the shoulder by a low-lying sniper. It took months to recover from his wound and he vowed it would never happen again. Keeping low, he crawled as close as he could to the turf and rocks and found himself in the thick of the forest off the track. At least he had cover here, with huge, close-growing tree trunks providing a sense of protection.

He lay in the undergrowth for some time deciding what to do next. He knew that the unexpected could always happen. He waited. At first he heard a whisper then a click of weaponry. Soon he saw two men, their heads covered in black beanies, faces blackened with paint and their bodies in dark camouflage uniforms. They could have been from any number of factions, Josefo didn't hazard a guess which group. As they walked past, turning from side to side and using the hand signals of the jungle, Josefo caught a glimpse of the man's black eyes. Then they were gone.

50

The young man Ko Tan had chosen was at the peak of his physical condition. His body was lean and the muscles of his arms and legs were primed. He was toned and tight. His mind was disciplined, the perfect solder who would follow any orders. He had worked for Ko Tan for ten years, his loyalty, even in these dark days, unquestionable. Ko Tan had hand-picked this youth from his team of security and was sure that he would execute a successful mission, the most difficult part of which would be to predict the whereabouts of Eve and be able to intersect at an appropriate point.

The young man looked down at his hands as he was waiting in front of Ko Tan. The older man also looked down.

'Your hands are strong and so is your mind. I have faith in you, Mak. You have shown your impeccable service to me over the years. I put the life of our visitor in your hands.'

Ko Tan and his young companion spent the next couple of hours studying the map and predicting Eve's whereabouts with the help of some random intelligence gained over the last few weeks.

'This woman is very valuable to us. There is

information still to tell.' Ko Tan knew that anything he said to Mak would be heeded to the letter. When he was very young, the death of his parents had temporarily put the boy into a kind of walking, non-listening and non-speaking coma. It had been several years before the boy had started talking — monosyllables at first — and then sentences. Ko Tan had known his parents, he'd promised them he'd look after the boy. It had taken so long for Mak to allow Ko Tan into his life, to trust another human being. And when he did — it was for life.

As Mak left the room and made his way down the path to his village, Ko Tan felt a jolt. The boy was young, the territory dangerous. Was he right to send him on this mission? If he died, Ko Tan would never forgive himself for defying the promise he made to Mak's parents. Could he trust this young man who had never been tested in such a way? But the boy was keen enough to do anything to further himself in the organization, to release his bonds of servitude to Ko Tan and take his rightful place in the party.

Ko Tan decided fate would take its course. He could do nothing more. He had set the wheels in motion, the mission would be the test. And Mak, would be the student.

51

She packed her few personal possessions into a bag and wiped the surface of the mahogany dressing table that had been part of the house for generations. Layers of dust and powder crept onto the sponge and left the wood gleaming in its old age. She looked up and into the large round mirror attached to the dressing table and saw a new face peering back. This face was different from the frightened girl child who had first entered Ko Tan's life to change it far more than he could ever guess. That girl had been small and hunched, her hair dank, always hanging over her face to hide her identity, her sadness. She had been thin, a servant glad to be taken under a wing, any wing that would not cause her more pain.

But this new face was a girl child no longer. Her hair was glossy black with a slight wave down to the small of her back, a fringe framing and softening the dark features of her face. This child was now a woman, with womanly curves men admired, and a radiance that was rarely acquired. But this one had acquired it and skilfully. She was pleased with her reflection, the no longer skinny arms, the cheeks full and rosy. Men had called her beautiful and Mya knew how to use that beauty when she needed it most.

A door behind her moved slightly in the mirror and she noticed almost imperceptibly the figure of Dottmar slipping back out. She smiled to herself as she closed the bag and wiped a smudge from the mirror with a tissue.

At the door she turned and surveyed what had been her home for the last seven years. She would not be alone any more, she would share in the life she had coveted all these years. She closed the door behind her and walked down the corridor to Ko Tan's room — the master bedroom of the house. Softly knocking on the door, she heard his voice say 'Come in,' as she entered his bedroom legitimately for the first time.

'Thank God, Mya — I have wanted you with me properly for so long. Come to me.'

He took her meagre belongings and placed them gently on the chest at the end of the bed. He guided her to the four-poster bed she had often slept in as a visitor. Now was different. She belonged and she was here to stay.

52

As she reached the compound short of breath and her heart bashing against the walls of her chest, Eve saw there were few people in the area. She looked up the hill and glimpsed San Wu on his balcony looking down at her. She saw her opportunity and forced her body and legs up the hill against their will.

When she reached the ancient, carved Chinese doors to his reception hall, she beat the wood with her hands and screamed, 'San Wu — I need to speak with you. Come now! Please!'

She waited, knowing he was there, he had seen her running towards him. She'd bruised her hands on the wooden carvings of the door before she realized San Wu was not going to make an appearance.

'Miss, you must go back to your cabin. San Wu cannot see you today.' It was one of San Wu's guards, the same one who had escorted her and given her water that second day.

'Yes but, he knows I'm here — he's not seeing anyone else is he? Can't he just come down and see me? Something terrible has happened!'

She let her legs give way underneath her and her body hit the ground next to the great double door. The world went upside down as her head banged against the hard floor and her body slumped to its side. She hit the wooden floor but she was still conscious, and in pain. Her swirling, incoherent thoughts raced to the coincidence of Josefo being away at the same time as her crop was destroyed but she fought against them. He had disappointed her before but he couldn't do something like this, so life threatening, against her whole reason for being here. Surely he wasn't that kind of man? She would know a man like that and never let him near her.

The view in front of her dazed eyes was clearing — from black to orange and to a clearer picture. Clearer vision meant clearer thought. If San Wu didn't want to see her, what did this mean? Was he protecting Josefo or was San Wu involved? Or, more possible, did he not care and was prepared to leave her out to dry like her besieged crop?

Whatever the reason, the outcome was the same — she was vulnerable and had to think of something fast. Her head was clearing and the dizziness subsiding as she pulled herself up using her battered hands to lever herself against the door handles. The guard had moved away, abandoning her just as his leader had done, cast her off as a used old sack, once useful but now worthless as the dust.

Getting to her feet, she stretched and straightened. Her nose was running and her cheeks were smeared and wet. She looked up to where her hill had been a flourishing garden and saw a figure walking toward her.

The lone figure approached and as it neared she saw it was Josefo. She jumped off the ledge and ran through the dust with her arms outstretched toward him, wanting to believe he was on her side. He encircled her with his own and the warmth of their breath caught in each other's ears before their lips met.

'Eve — what has happened? I passed your crop as I was walking back. What is going on?'

'San Wu won't see me. He's shut me off!' As she spoke she realized Josefo had started early that morning with five other men, and she looked at him with new eyes. She saw a brave but shattered man, his empty eyes hiding the sorrow beneath.

'Where is your patrol?'

'You were not the only one being ambushed, Eve. We were followed but I do not believe it was an enemy. I do not know who exactly, but my heart is not happy. All the others are lost. The men who killed them were disguised — unrecognizable. But they were militia.'

'It was the group San Wu warned us about. The same group who destroyed my crop! It must have been!' Eve searched his face for agreement but received a blank stare.

'Why will San Wu not see you? What did you want to say to him?' Josefo looked toward the balcony where San Wu sometimes strolled.

'I was worried about you and I wanted to know where he'd sent you. But you're back — and safe. I need to think about what I have to do.' Eve added this more to herself than to him as her sentence trailed off.

'Eve, why was your crop destroyed — no matter who did it?' He searched her face for the answer. And added: 'Shh, speak softly. Ears are around.'

'Josefo, I lied. To you and San Wu. Those crops were not opium but a hybrid breed of tobacco that looks like opium. I was buying time to get him to talk to me.'

'That was not wise, Eve. As you have seen. It is San Wu who has found out. We must pretend we do not know. There is nothing else we can do.' He moved away.

'I will arrange a meeting. We must see what can be

done, what he has planned next. We must be prepared for a counter attack.'

Josefo didn't want to confide his bewildered feelings to Eve. He had to present the brave soldier's face to her and especially to San Wu. He must be able to offer an explanation for the events from his viewpoint and make San Wu believe he didn't know who was responsible.

Josefo beckoned the guard who had been loitering by the large wooden doors. Josefo leant forward and whispered something to the other man who disappeared inside the auditorium.

'Do you think he'll see us?' whispered Eve.

'Shh — just be patient.'

A short while later, the guard reappeared at the doors and motioned to Josefo to come forward. He did so but, as he approached the open doors, he turned to Eve and placed his forefinger over his mouth.

He turned toward the doorway and entered, clanging the large doors behind him as the image of Eve disappeared. He was faced with the long red carpet, the walk towards the dais and the sight of San Wu already seated on his red velvet throne. This time his delicate feet still encased in their slippers, were resting on a gold velvet cushion with four tassels.

'What is the meaning of this intrusion? I am the one to call the meetings, not you, or your woman. You should control her more.' San Wu turned in his chair away from Josefo, feigning an upset like a child who can't have chocolate.

'I am so sorry, sir. I tried to deter her but she is strong and might suspect something unusual if I don't meet with you to discuss the situation. '

'Alright, but you are here now and you called this meeting. But it is I who need to talk to you. I believe you had problems on your patrol. Do not worry about it, these things happen.' Josefo flinched at the curt dismissal of the deaths of his comrades.

'Now the woman's crop — this is what you want to know, am I correct?' San Wu stared at Josefo, waiting for an answer.

'Yes, I am confused. I thought the plants were fine and protected from alien patrols. What went wrong?'

'Yes, it is a strange affair. I know that the very workers who have been tilling those fields for the last months have sabotaged their own project. You cannot believe these peasants! No matter. What is important is that I did not get a chance to see the growth of the woman's crop so I have no belief in her. I am not surprised the peasants turned against her.'

'No belief in what, sir? Surely you saw the crop from your window. You could see the growth was phenomenal! And sir, I cannot believe these peasants have betrayed her and the project they have been working on for so long. No!' said Josefo.

'There is no place for argument. I decided and I acted. I saw nothing of this phenomenal crop. Do not tell me what I did not see, my boy, or you too will feel my wrath. Be careful and keep your eyes on your goal, remember only I can get you there. I believe the woman is lying. The only reason I can think of is to destroy me and everything I have strived for.'

'But San Wu, sir, how can she do that? She has no power, not like you. You have it all, the power and the presence to create and destroy as you wish. Not this woman.' Josefo tried to placate San Wu's rising anger but felt himself getting further out to sea. 'Please sir, do not think this. It is not the case. She was trying hard.'

'Trying is not what I want. You must succeed, my boy, there is no failure. Learn from that.' San Wu raised his body from the throne and walked with difficulty to the large curtain at the back of the room. He turned and stared at Josefo.

'Listen, boy, and listen carefully. This woman is no longer wanted here. She must go back to the city and you must take her. Are you willing?'

'Yes, I am your servant — whatever you ask, sir, I will do.'

'Good. I want you to prepare her for departure for the city, leaving tomorrow. Tell her anything but just get her out of here. I cannot stand the sight of her or her Robinson name.' Josefo was surprised by San Wu's sudden attack. But his role was not to question, his brief was to follow orders. He turned to leave the auditorium. Just as he was about to exit through the large doors, San Wu called after him.

'Give her back this useless book.' San Wu threw the diary which landed at Josefo's feet. 'By the way, my boy, on your way to the city, kill her.'

53

I t had been four days the first time. This time, the return to the city would be nowhere near as torturous as the journey to San Wu's village. The walking would be short — the way clear and bright. They had only to walk a few miles to get over the bridge before they would be picked up by jeep and then the plane for the rest of the journey. The details were planned, the rendezvous with the pilot and driver organized. Josefo calculated two days this time.

The night San Wu had given his order, Josefo had returned to their hut with a heart so heavy he had trouble putting one foot in front of the other. To ask him this was cruel, San Wu knew he had feelings for the woman. He knew, feelings could not get in the way of duty and the fight for the cause. It would certainly not be pleasant, he would hate everything about it. Perhaps he could separate his feelings for the woman and it would not be so bad. The great man had promised him leadership and power but at what cost? He didn't have to think for too long to realize that his whole life had been heading towards this point, and that he must take this opportunity. It would never happen again. But he allowed the sadness to creep into his heart.

He had not been long in the meeting with the great

man, and had entered the front door to the smells of rogan josh and daal bhat. Eve's culinary abilities had developed and she now had a range of dishes she could muster at a moment's notice. She wanted to know what San Wu had said. Josefo told her that nothing had transpired, that San Wu had put on one of his acts and then offered nothing. She had been satisfied with the story though she was still angry about what had happened to her crop.

'He told me one thing though, Eve, that you should know. He would like you to return to the city and I am to escort you there. We must prepare for departure tomorrow.' He waited for this news to enter her consciousness.

'Leave — but this is great news! I never would have thought this would happen. But ... why so easy, Josefo? Does he not want anything more from me — has he everything he needs to know now? And what about my answers? He has not even seen me again to discuss the past.'

'I do not know, Eve. All I know is that this is what he wants and it must be carried out.'

'But can't you find out — or let me! I will go to him tomorrow for an audience. He will see me, surely, if I am to leave soon after. He can tell me more about my father ...' Eve's face looked hopeful as she spooned another piece of food into her mouth.

'No, it is not to be. He is not having any more audiences. Just believe that we must leave.'

'But I have so many questions still.'

'No, leave it. Eat.'

He was not often abrupt with her and she was surprised. But her questions stopped and they ate in silence. Later as she lit the candle beside the bed, Eve looked into Josefo's eyes. He took her hand in response, led her to the bed and laid her head gently on the pillow. His kiss was gentle as his tongue explored the inside of her soft pink flesh, tickling.

'I need to speak first.' She waited until he was looking at her.

'Yes — speak first.'

'Are we to do much walking this time, over the hills and bridges?'

'Less than last time. We have planned for pickup after only a day of walking. Why does this concern you? You are very strong and have not had to worry since your work on the crops?'

Eve paused, flushed, her heart beating with a fear only dimly remembered. But now that fear was tinged with something she could not name. Something exciting. She took Josefo's hand and placed it on her soft belly, circling it around catching his fingers with her own.

'Because I'm pregnant. We are to have our own child, Josefo.'

Their passion that night was unsurpassed. Their bodies merged into a symbiosis of lips, tongues and a fusion of souls. It reminded him of the first time they had been together, only this time it was he who was in control. He took her soft body and melded it into his own, showing it the way and making it yield to his desire. Arms, hands, legs and fingers played together in unison. As their passion lit their senses, they came to rest amidst the ruins of bedclothes and pillows scattered about the room. He stroked her cheek and kissed her gently once again. He formed the words on his lips before he uttered them for the first time.

'I love you, my Eve.'

54

Her body was feeling its age, in the mornings she groaned with pain as she rolled to one side of the bed and then off the side to her feet. She looked down at her legs feeling as if they belonged to someone else. She could twist her toes when her brain told them but they still felt detached from the rest of her body. As she raised the rest of her weight off the bed, it shifted to her heart as she remembered what was happening around her.

Dottmar was no longer young, she had realized that long ago. Slowly she had seen her glossy black hair turn grey. Ko Tan's had turned grey also but that was not important for men. Women had to keep their beauty, otherwise their wiles and tactics became less effective. She had noticed the diminishing passion in her marriage but the presence of the girl had destabilized her comfort. Dottmar had a permanent pain in her stomach, in its inner reaches where the juices themselves were forming, she could feel the turbulence and knew the headaches would soon follow. She had a home but she was no longer comfortable here. She could go nowhere without bumping into Mya, seeing her in the corridors telling the other servants what to do. She was no longer the maid of the house. She was openly living with Ko Tan. Yet after all these years, as his wife, Dottmar knew she had to remain in a dominant position for as long as she could. With no support, it would not be easy but what was the alternative? With her sons now gone from the house, Abau dead and Than not close enough to be concerned with his mother's petty domestic woes, she had to rely on herself.

Some days, for no reason except to make herself feel as lifted as a lark, she would take a leisurely bath, and dress herself in her traditional silk magenta sari with its pleats of orange, peach and frangipani. It was a slow deliberate process, as if she were creating the layers of her life and arranging them the way they should be on her skin. It gave her a sense of calm so that, once she had left her room, she was ready to present herself to the day. She walked to the terrace where Mya normally had breakfast waiting for Dottmar and Ko Tan. Today was different.

'Ah Dottmar, please join us,' said Mya, not rising from her seat at the table next to Ko Tan. She had a smile on her face, an expression Dottmar had not seen before. She didn't like it. The situation was not unexpected but somehow she had always thought Ko Tan would continue to have respect for her in this home they shared. She felt her face drain, her heart palpitated and her hands went clammy. She became aware of a growing anger in her belly.

'I will take my breakfast on my balcony. Please arrange for it to be prepared. You know what I like.' Dottmar turned and retreated in the direction from which she had emerged.

In her room, she felt panic clouding her vision. She hit the pillow and sobbed. Soon, she straightened herself, and stroked the silk of the sari on her thighs. She would reclaim her palace, the girl had to go.

55

It had been a tiring day. San Wu had not pronounced any judgments on wrongdoers for a long time. It sapped his ever-expiring energy. This one had been particularly difficult. So many in one day was hard, after so long. San Wu rested his body on his ornate four-poster bed covered in a gossamer mattress and organza bedspread. He didn't often reflect on the day once it was gone but the peasants' faces had remained with him. He had only killed one by his own hand, personal executions had stopped long ago. The young soldier, Josefo — it would be a great test for him. He had performed well today. Testing under pressure was a success — he had passed, though he was not aware of it. Belief and faith was everything. He was a good choice for the task at hand. But San Wu no longer needed a successor.

San Wu was not sure the young man was ready to be trusted. Once a man became involved with a western woman, there was no saying what would be the outcome. It could only lead to the death of at least one of the parties. But San Wu had to ask himself, was she as white as she had claimed? An interesting theory. The diary had been useful to a certain degree though he knew more of the background than could be told in that small book, he had been able to piece together some cogs in the wheels of Alex's life. He knew of Ko Tan and Dottmar, Alex's old school friends. But Alexandra? That was a surprise even to him. That a woman could continue to weave an intriguing web around her family into the next generation long after her husband and son were dead — this was proven by the diary. He had not been aware she was so clever. He could have shared more with Eve. Yet she had everything she needed to complete the puzzle if she thought about it. The last pieces were staring her in the face. 'Information is King' he thought to himself. It would come to pass.

He prepared his pipe as he readied himself for bed, the four-poster was waiting for him as usual. His deep breaths inhaled the precious smoke that would send him to a dream planet of ecstasy until morning. He closed his eyes to let the dream take him.

56

Eve had noticed the weather changing. Since her time in the jungle, most days had been overcast but warm in the mornings, greyer throughout the day, culminating in a torrential downpour by afternoon. She was pleased how well she had acclimatized and remembered her experience in the hotel that first day she had met Dottmar. Then, she felt stifled, trapped, almost strangled by the heat and thought she would never get used to it. She found in the mountains that as long as her clothes were lightweight she managed to feel comfortable despite being wet by the rain or covered in sweat. The perspiration or precipitation dried off in a few minutes. Long gone was the need for makeup and good hair days. But lately she had noticed the heat building early in the morning with no sign of rain to cool the thick tracks in the compound. It was in this overheating season that the two made preparations to leave, packing the few belongings they would carry across the mountain to the main track and a waiting jeep.

San Wu had still not required an audience since he told them they were to leave. They were at the edge of the compound. A few of the men gathered around to say their shy farewells. Eve shook some hands and noted the guard of San Wu's main hall giving Josefo an especially warm handshake. Josefo received a few small gifts, placed them inside his combat jacket pockets before motioning to Eve to move along the path and away from the village. As she turned around to see the last of the few villagers who had bid them goodbye, she looked up at San Wu's balcony and fancied she saw him there lingering in the shadows. She couldn't see the detail but imagined a last glimpse of his small stature standing at the doorway in his Chinese slippers, their pinkness shining through the curtains.

She tried to speak but found her voice had left her, to be replaced by a mass in her throat that rose up and refused to be subdued. Her eyes brimmed with tears. She was facing away from the crowd and a good way up from Josefo so she let the tears come and the pain of those who had been sacrificed overpower her. She reflected on her time in the village. What had she accomplished? She had lost the diary, and had no final information from San Wu. He had not returned the diary but he had given her some background to the story she so desperately required. But there must be more than that? She had survived — that was something, though would she return to the city with information she could have gained in another way? There must be something missing, something more she could do?

Eve moved ahead of Josefo as he was saying farewell to the crowd. She needed time alone to compose herself. She did not like being watched when having an emotional outburst. Though this was hardly an outburst, she told herself, but more a release of a feeling that had been growing for some time, longer than she could have imagined. With the feeling about to overcome her she needed physical exertion to help dissipate some of the rage or torment or whatever it was. She didn't have a name for it. Since the pills had run out she had noticed an intensity about herself, her awareness, even her vision, was clearer. No tremors or blackouts. It wasn't something she tried to understand, it simply existed as it had never done so before.

As she forced one leg in front of the other, now lean, sinewy and strong, she covered her belly with her brown hands. She fancied she could feel it growing each minute. There was no pharmacy tester to be found in the jungle but she knew. She knew that bloated, heavy feeling, the thickness of the body that consumed her. It was long ago but it was a feeling a woman never forgot. Every woman knew what was happening to her own body. For Eve, it was a memory, come back to the forefront of her consciousness to yet again try to tear her away from herself, lose herself in the past and future. But not this time. This time she cupped the warm belly, heavy with life in her strong supple hands, willing it to exist, to come upon her, take over her, be her. This time she welcomed it in and she would love this thing that she created. This time she would create, not kill.

57

Josefo monitored Eve, watching her movements, noting any lack of strength or speed. How ironic, he thought, remembering he had acted in a similar way the first time around although for completely different reasons. He thought about himself back then in a time which seemed so long ago and yet was only a matter of months. He felt different, not only in his heart but in his soul. He was a shifting sand that had come to rest in a different place, a place which would hold him safely for the rest of his life. There was something about that safe feeling and knew that a feeling of home is not necessarily a place. He knew it was a person. He had found home and he was going to stay. His thoughts were jolted by the realization of his task on the walk back. He couldn't put it out of his mind and knew that somehow he would have to make a decision he had never made for anyone, even himself. Choose loyalty and ambition — or an option outside his reality; the frightening unknown.

Most of his life he had only ever known how to look after himself, his childhood years were a thing of the past. He'd had other responsibilities, looking after his young sibling. But that had been so long ago. It was a dim memory, a shadow recollection that paralleled his shadow universe, something all his subsequent life he had tried to forget. For some reason the image of that young girl leapt to his mind now all those years later. The dark cloud of his subconscious followed and his mood dropped to the level of the stream below them at the foot of the mountain.

He had faced dilemmas in his life before, this would be another. He would rise above the choice and know the option would resolve itself and lift him to a higher level. It would be difficult but if freedom was the choice then there was no choice.

He had never come this close. How did one ever really know? As a man you were never sure, only if you had complete trust in the woman and how could that be? Josefo remembered once he had journeyed to a village where he had stayed for a time and known a woman there. He had returned — it was years later, maybe three or four — and had hardly remembered the village, much less the woman. But he had seen a child there, the child's eyes a mirror of his own. It had transfixed him, the feeling of seeing his own eyes in another random being whom he'd never known he might meet. The child had looked away, run to his mother who had viewed Josefo suspiciously, but with recognition.

He knew the place a child might hold in his life if he chose to envelop it. He let the idea sit in his subconscious for a while. Left it there. He liked it.

The first few hours walking had not been arduous. Both were strong walkers and Eve was now more used to the extreme weather conditions. She paced herself while he walked behind a few paces, more deliberately than she. By late afternoon, Josefo realized she could probably not walk further so decided to make camp at a familiar night harbor. The place was one he'd used many times; chosen for its protection from wind and rain, and securely surrounded by mid-height trees making a natural enclave. There was a small low-level cave to the rear of the camp which they used instead of pitching the tent. Eve walked to it and prepared the ground for them while Josefo checked the perimeter.

Once Josefo had secured the area and their cave was prepared, he started to build a fire. He liked a fire, even when it wasn't cold. They still needed the heat to boil water and the temperature of the evenings often dropped.

He dived into a pocket of his pack and pulled out what had become their favorite drink. Having managed to accumulate a few bottles over the last weeks he had put a couple into his pack for emergencies. Eve had developed a taste for the liquid she had formerly called medicine. Something about her taste perception had changed since her time in the jungle and the whiskey flowed smoothly down her throat, calming her.

Dinner was a kind of vegetable rice mixture, pre-dried and mixed with hot water to produce something halfway edible with a few pieces of protein thrown in.

They felt safe in their cave and the firelight dazzled their already soporific eyes. Eve closed hers and leant back against her makeshift bed letting her thoughts race. She thought more of the past than the future. The past flirted with her since she had known about her pregnancy. The future would take care of itself. She tried to make sense of recollections, the actions that had caused the destruction of her marriage. Would it have happened anyway, she wondered?

Josefo was tending the fire and by now had taken a couple of long pulls of the whiskey. Eve had become used to drinking out of the bottle and decided the fluid had a distinctly different flavor that way.

'Another?' Josefo offered her the bottle. She took it

from him and put it to her lips for a sip of the liquor.

'Josefo? I've told you a little about my marriage but you've never asked more.'

'It is for you to share, not for me to ask. Would you like to tell me about him?'

'Not about him, really. But about something. Something not so nice to tell. Or to hear.'

This intrigued him. This woman had always been circumspect in her sharing of her life, he had not questioned it. He just loved what they had together. No past, no future.

'Go on.'

'Roger was desperate for a child — I wasn't. But I became pregnant.' Eve looked at him, waiting for a response. When she had none, she continued.

'I was studying, was busy and had other goals. I wanted to wait. It was an accident but he was overjoyed when he found out. Only I couldn't go through with it. There was something stopping me. I destroyed our baby before it had a chance for life. He never forgave me. That's why he left.'

Josefo turned to look at her and saw the sadness in her face.

'This does not happen in our culture — not that early anyway. Often it comes later when the parent causes the death of the child. But that is called murder or worse. What is this called when you do not allow your child to live?' He produced one of his intense stares which she could not escape.

'It's called abortion. That's the old-fashioned name anyway. Now it's called a termination.'

Josefo thought about the women in his life and wondered if any of them would have done such a thing if they'd had the choice. He guessed it wouldn't be safe in his country, it would be too risky. Perhaps the women did do it — he didn't know, had never thought to ask. What of his own mother who had borne several children with little to feed them? Most died without help anyway. Except for Josefo and Marinda. Would she have thought of destroying his life before breath? He looked at Eve.

'This was a hard thing to do? It caused sadness?'

'Yes.'

'But it was your choice, yes?'

'I think so but I still felt guilty about it. I should have thought more about Roger. I think I was very selfish.' Eve looked into the fire.

'It is a great thing to realize something about yourself that is not perfect. Not all of us can do it.'

Josefo felt sad, that familiar tightness in the throat and heat behind the eyes. He looked across at Eve whose face was highlighted by the flames of the fire, lit up warm and pink. Her eyes were glistening. He felt close to her now, closer than he had felt to anyone and knew that he could not carry out San Wu's orders, his bite of the promotional cherry could never be. Strangely, the sadness in his chest began to subside and he knew he had to share something with Eve.

'You have said to me before that I do not talk about myself. I realize this but it is hard for me you must understand.' He waited for her acknowledgement to continue. 'I have been on my own for a lot of my life, have had to fend for myself, nurture myself as best I could. I could never trust anyone. Until now.'

He swallowed, anticipating the story he was about to tell — the story which had never been told.

'Do you remember on that journey up to the mountains all those months ago? We had talked by the fire. Not unlike now.' He waited.

'Yes I remember we had a chat. You talked a little about your family, your sister, Marinda wasn't it?'

'What did I tell you, do you remember?'

'You said she had been taken from the farm. That your parents knew about it but that you had found a hiding spot for her. The soldiers had found her anyway. You seemed to blame yourself for something you could not have controlled.'

Josefo swallowed again.

'I lied to you. When the soldiers arrived, my parents called and called for her. But somehow she seemed to know what was to happen. She had found her own hiding place in that small corner of the chicken coop but on the way she told me where she was, she trusted me with her life. They would never find her, she said. It was foolproof, she had hidden from others many times before. Lead them away, she said. They are not after you.

'I walked out into the yard just as the soldiers were dismounting from the trucks. I could see the many writhing black bundles in the back of the truck. Ours was not the first village they had sacked.

'I have thought about that moment so many times since and wished they had taken me instead that day. As they approached me, I pointed directly to Marinda's small corner at the far end of the chicken coop. They would never have found her but I showed them, Eve, I gave up my own sister to slavery, isolation from her home and family forever. So you see. I deserve nothing.'

He said no more but buried his head in his hands and wept.

Eve had never seen a man cry. She had to admit that she did not know Josefo well, but she had not imagined she'd be a witness to this. It unnerved her but warmed her to him. He was human and sensitive underneath the mask.

She moved over to his side, put her arm around his

shoulder and pulled his head into her own.

'You've felt a lot of pain over the years, haven't you?' she asked not knowing if she would receive an answer.

'I have been searching for her for years. Finding her will be my redemption. I am sure of it. I will be happy only when we are together again.'

Eve wasn't convinced this would be the case after so many years and separate experiences lived by them both. But she didn't want to dampen Josefo's spirits any further. She was there to soothe him in his sadness.

He stopped weeping and they lay down together on the sleeping mats she had prepared in the small cave. He had spoken more but the words were incoherent so she just said yes and let him talk.

Their makeshift bed was comfortable, their thermal mats took the chill off the ground, the sleeping bags protecting them from insects. She had a fitful sleep, aware that Josefo had also had a disturbed night.

She had just fallen under the night's magic when she felt a stirring in the bag close to her shoulder. The sleeping bags had been joined together to provide a single covering across both their bodies. Eve felt the stirring grow to a feeling of cold against her skin and she woke to find herself staring into the face of a snake. The creature looked drowsy. Perhaps she had been asleep next to it for most of the night and had triggered it awake with a shift of her body.

Eve had learnt enough of the jungle to know that the most colorful creatures were not always the most dangerous. The firelight showed that this one was green with very few markings. She managed to unzip her bag at the side. Just as she had completed this not so simple task, Josefo woke up. In an instant, he had the snake by the jaw with his other hand on its body. He jumped from the bag with the snake in his hands. He had freed himself from the bag but did not see the last logs of the fire from the night before. As he looked into the eye of the snake trying to break its neck, his foot smashed against a log and he fell to the ground directly on top of the snake.

Eve heard the heavy thud and saw his dark shadow lying in the dirt. She dashed to him in the dark and turned him over. He had killed the snake but in the light of the dying fire she saw two clear holes in the skin of his throat. He was gasping. She couldn't think what to do. Just as she was remembering to immobilize and bandage, Josefo moved his arm and reached into his coat pocket. His hand emerged holding a battered dusty notebook — the diary Eve had so missed. She took it from him. His hand moved up as he pulled a chain from around his neck. He placed the half medallion in her hand, the other half of the one Eve had seen on the neck of Ko Tan's maid, Mya.

'Find her. Tell her I loved her. And tell her I am so sorry.' Josefo struggled to get the words out. Eve put the chain and pendant into her pocket and ran back to her pack to get a bandage.

She returned to find him there by the fire, his life gone with the snake dead by his side.

58

Eve had been walking for more than two days. She had seen two mornings and two black nights, felt the cold of aloneness and had aching legs and feet. She knew if she had been walking for more than two days, she was lost. Josefo had been definite that in two days they would reach the airstrip and plane which would take them back to Rangoon and home.

By now she was used to the physical pain. She had ditched most of the gear so was travelling light with only her pack to worry about. The emotional pain was not so easy to combat. After the death of Josefo, she found herself in shock, though she didn't know it at the time. She felt an anxiety like no other but the tears never came. An instinct of survival kicked in as her brain calculated what needed to be done. She was practical and reacted fast to the tragedy yet her heart remained unaffected. It was only on the second night when she camped inside the loving entwining branches of a banyan tree that her senses started to move and she was overwhelmed by sorrow. The tears came for this man, whom she knew had loved her. This was so new to Eve that her grieving was partly for herself, that she had lost something she had not believed could exist. She knew he was real, but he was gone.

She felt safe inside the arms of the enormous tree but knew as soon as she stepped outside its protective embrace, she would be in danger. Yet there was no choice but to dive into the unknown and pursue the track to a place in the future.

*

It was the sobbing — of a woman he could tell — that alerted him to turn in a different direction. His march had been relentless. He had covered much ground in a relatively short time. This was a new and valuable lead. He could smell his quarry and he knew he was close. His heart beat a little faster and he increased the pace of his steps to match. This was it, at last he was to complete his mission.

As the sobbing grew louder, he slowed down and walked towards a large banyan tree which had been emitting the sounds. Dawn had just broken and the light of the morning was not yet bright. The air had a sallow complexion. As he approached the tree, his foot hit a branch. He cursed under his breath as he noticed the crying stop and silence take its place.

There was no need for quiet now so he approached the entrance to the tree and stood in front of a woman with her mouth open and tears on her face. His large frame blotted out the merging light.

Eve looked up at the shadowy stranger and amidst her misery felt a remembered sensation, fear.

The man was Burmese, young, tall, and athletic. His face was impassive as he looked at her unspeaking. She looked back with a dispassionate stare and then didn't move.

'My name is Mak. Ko Tan has sent me. Do not worry, Daw Eve, I will get you home.'

59

As she stepped into the courtyard of the once-grand house, Eve remembered the first time she had seen it. It seemed so long ago. She had looked at the house then with fresh, unknowing eyes and had seen decay and age. She looked at the house now and saw dignity, past glory — a pride in its age, and survival. The weeds were not quite as overgrown as they once were, perhaps someone had pulled out these living monuments to waste and ugliness. The copse of trees was still there and the front door was slightly ajar, perhaps waiting for the return of someone from the past.

This time it was Eve returning and she was greeted by Dottmar at the entrance to the courtyard. The older woman ran to meet Eve, her arms outstretched, the edge of her red sari catching the breeze. Dottmar's arms encircled Eve's body with an all-encompassing warmth — something Eve had not felt from another woman. Her loving embrace took Eve by surprise. Both women had tears in their eyes as they buried their heads in each other's necks.

'Eve, it is so good to have you back. You were missed.' Dottmar held the younger woman close, not wanting to release her hold. She moved away and looked into Eve's eyes. Her expression softened and when she spoke again, she spoke close to Eve's ear.

'You look radiantly beautiful, my Eve. You have new life within you.'

When her eyes met Dottmar's, she looked away.

'Dottmar, thank you — I have so much to tell. But I may still be in danger.' Eve returned Dottmar's hug and then they walked side by side with arms interlocked into the great hall and to the library.

Ko Tan rose from his library chair and greeted Eve with restrained enthusiasm.

'Eve — we are so glad you are safe. We can thank Mak for that.' Ko Tan greeted her warmly.

'There are a lot of others I would also need to thank for that, Ko Tan!'

He motioned for Eve to sit as she spoke, piecing together most of the last months of her life in the village. Both Dottmar and Ko Tan listened to her story, once in a while stealing a look at each other above Eve's animated face.

'Ko Tan, we are in danger. This leader, San Wu, is dangerously obsessive. There is no predicting what he will do next. I think he wants me dead.'

'Eve, if he had wanted you dead, would you not be dead already? He had plenty of opportunity in the hills from what you tell us. We know of his methods, of course. This sort of man's reputation spreads far. He is dangerous and unpredictable, I agree. But why would he want to kill you?' Eve shifted in her chair.

'I tricked him into believing that I was able to grow a hyperplant poppy that would outsell his crop. But the plant I was cultivating was merely the domestic tobacco. I think he found out. I think he lost face and wants me dead. I fear that his men have followed me and will come for all of us now that I'm back at the house.'

'Indeed,' said Ko Tan, 'but you have done nothing to him. Do you have information that he may have given you — something that may be useful in other ways?'

'I showed him Dad's diary — he demanded it from me. But he said he knew everything that was in the diary already. He told me a bit about my father and grandfather's early days and how he knew them both. He said I still had relatives living in Rangoon.'

Ko Tan and Dottmar looked away.

'Did he say who they were — reveal their identities?'

'No, he said no more about it. Do you know anything about these people? Do they exist?'

'Yes Eve — we do,' Dottmar said.

'Ko Tan and I were the closest people to your father for many years. There are things about his life — and people — he has hidden from you for reasons only he could know. Can you not guess?'

There were so many thoughts in Eve's head she had not focused on what was right in front of her all along. She still didn't get it. She had to hear it from them in their own words.

'I don't understand, Dottmar. What are you saying?'

There was a rustling at the door and just as Eve asked her question, Mya entered the library. Eve's heart jumped with the recognition of Josefo's image she now saw in the young girl's face. The eyes and nose were the same, that same intensity of stare. Just the shape of the face surrounded by long hair was different.

'Yes — we all know what you are saying, Dottmar,' said Mya with a confidence Eve found unsettling.

'This has nothing to do with you!'

'Why not tell the stupid bitch what everyone else knows?' Mya glared at Eve.

'Mya — stop!' This time Ko Tan spoke quietly.

'Even Abau knew the night he took her ...' Mya stopped short.

'Mya — you tried to blame Eve for Abau's death — how could you! We have been so kind to you ...,' said Ko Tan.

'Like a well-kept dog. And I have had enough.'

Dottmar walked up to Ko Tan.

'Ko Tan — you must take her away from here and never return — the both of you. What we know will soon be common knowledge. Your life will be in danger.'

Ko Tan turned to Eve. His head bowed.

'You have wanted the truth for a long time. I was there the night San Wu killed your grandfather. Yes, he was the organizer ... and I helped him do it. After Alexandra told us about the meeting place. Poi Trang had nothing to do with it. He has been wanting to know who helped San Wu for years. Eve, it is not you who is in danger from San Wu. You are of no use to him now. It is I they want —Poi Trang and San Wu. I am the one in danger.'

'But Ko Tan. San Wu told me that the boy who helped kill Raoul was his own son — from a union with his aya. Ko Tan ...?' Eve looked at Ko Tan.

He turned away.

'I am not proud of that night. It is one of my many regrets.' Ko Tan paused.

'If I do not leave here tonight, it will not only be myself I will harm. Mya, get your things — we are leaving.' For a moment, Mya's face twisted into anger. Then she was calm. She turned around to leave the room, all her energy spent.

'Mya, wait,' Eve said, reaching into her pocket. 'I have something for you. Something from your brother, Josefo.'

Mya stopped and turned, her face expressionless. She held out her hand to take the half medallion and held it up against her own — forming the whole shape of a coin. Tears formed in her eyes.

'He loved you till the end — he wanted you to know. He died ... saying he was sorry he could not find you to say how he loved you still.' Eve stepped back and watched the young woman's face twist.

'Josefo.' Mya said the word looking at the trinket with, Eve thought, loving eyes.

'Josefo? Loved me? It is he who forced me into this life of servitude. I have been wanting to find him for years and now he is dead! I can never tell him how much I hated him! He can rot in hell and you with him.' She threw the pendant to the floor and ran from the room. Ko Tan raised his face to her departing figure and in that moment, Dottmar knew that not only was she rid of the young village girl who had usurped her role in the house, but that she had lost her husband.

'It was so long ago, Eve — but I have learned that the past never leaves us. All we can hope is that we can survive it and move on,' Dottmar said.

Dottmar and Eve watched as Ko Tan guided Mya to the door, dragging his meagre belongings behind him. Eve watched as they disappeared from view.

'We were so young, Eve. Two kids really. And two kids we remained even when we had one of our own. We loved each other, Eve — I did not betray him.'

'Are you talking about Ko Tan, Dottmar? What do you mean?'

'I am speaking of your father, Alex. We were married and had a child, Eve. You.'

The blood drained from Eve's face. Dottmar took her hands and helped her to sit in the library chair where she had first conversed with Ko Tan about her father's childhood.

'I never realized, Dottmar. Now I can see it as clearly as day ...'

She remembered the few times her father had mentioned her mother. She'd died in an accident, he'd said. That's all. No details. The only photo of her mother was of a woman in the mid-distance, two arms holding a baby, the blond father smiling by her side. There had been so many questions. The questions he could not or would not answer. Questions she didn't even know to ask. And now she had answers.

Eve looked up, her face streaming with tears.

'I am sorry you had to find out like this, it is not fair.'

'It's just the years of not knowing — I feel tricked in a way. Not by you, but by my father.'

'He had his reasons, do not blame him — it was a different era. Just remember, he was no coward. He was a visionary.'

'But why did you not come to Australia — with us?' Dottmar looked away.

'I was different then. I still had dreams I could help my country. Ko Tan made it sound so good. I just couldn't leave my home to live in a foreign place so far away. And Alex was different. He'd lost that inspiration — he no longer belonged here. I thought I still did. I made a mistake, Eve.'

She looked up at Dottmar and saw her own eyes reflected. She knew why she had felt so comfortable in this country, with these people. They were her people.

'There's still time, Dottmar ...' Dottmar smiled.

'And your child, Eve?'

'I will call him Alex.'

Epilogue

T *o my Alex, finally I have found you to tell you the truth you so deserve to know ... I wanted to meet you and tell you this in person. That is why I have invited you to come here. You must come!*

I loved Raoul, your father, so much at first I could hardly bear it. We were both religious but that did not stop him from impregnating our aya. He said he loved her. After everything we had been to each other. How can a wife recover from that? No — the baby was not you, my darling. I could not bear the knowledge of this other child. I banned both mother and baby from the house. She brought him up in a village not far away, called him Ko Tan. No matter. Raoul never forgave me, he hated me after that. I had to leave in the end. I found a man to love me, my sweet. He did, despite himself. He was opposed to everything Raoul stood for but I loved San Wu, and he loved me back. The heart has no mercy, my darling, no allegiances. One day you will come to know that. Raoul had started his Freedom Party, became known as the Tiger. I knew a lot about it, my dear, but I never realized that San Wu wanted to get to Raoul through me. How could I know this? Do not hate me for it, please, my sweet. By mistake (I swear it was), I showed San Wu where Raoul secretly met with his band of rebels. Even before that, it had been our own secret hiding place. I called them rebels, my darling, because they went against the government — and that is not right, is it? They called themselves saviors of our people. Can it be true? San Wu soon introduced me to his protégé called Ko Tan! What a terrible coincidence! I wanted nothing to do with the boy. He was a blasphemy, a blight on the family. San Wu had known all along who this boy was. Then, one night, San Wu led a group into the jungle to Raoul's secret location. He hunted Raoul down, like an animal — he could not escape. San Wu made Ko Tan put the final bullet in his own father's head — how ironic! I know it is sad, my darling, but what could I have done. He killed my first love. I can't believe it was my fault. They killed him, my Raoul, my tiger, my love. I never wanted that, my darling, you must believe me. I did not know any of this would come to pass. I just loved two men. I know I am not wise. I have been foolhardy and unthinking. I was desperately unhappy — I could not face you back then. After what happened. I couldn't tell you — you would have hated me. What you must make of me! I am writing this to you so that you can forgive me for the past, and still love me or at least the memory of me. I will die very soon, not by my own hand, but a scourge on my body that cannot be controlled. This is my punishment, my dear one. I never knew you, my son, but I hope you can one day come to love me as I have always loved you ... perhaps in death we will be joined again ...

Your adoring mother, Alexandra

ABOUT THE AUTHOR

Robin Bower is a writer and accredited editor with more than 20 years publishing experience in Australia and overseas. She was publisher/managing editor for a magazine in Hong Kong, where she reported on the diamond industry in Asia and Europe. She taught Writing, Editing and Publishing at Curtin University, Perth, and has had almost 50 articles published in publications based in Hong Kong, Perth and Melbourne. Robin holds a Master of Creative Writing from the University of Canberra. She lives with her husband in Perth, Western Australia. *Beyond Home* is her first novel.

Robin's second novel, set in Perth and Afghanistan, will be available soon.

For more information, see www.robinbower.com.au.

Printed in Great Britain
by Amazon